WAVERING

NAGARU TANIGAWA

YEN
ON
NEW YORK

The Wavering of Haruhi Suzumiya
Nagaru Tanigawa

Translation by Paul Starr
Cover art by Noizi Ito

This book is a work of fiction. Names, characters, places, and incidents are the product
of the author's imagination or are used fictitiously. Any resemblance to actual events,
locales, or persons, living or dead, is coincidental.

Suzumiya Haruhi No Douyou
©Nagaru Tanigawa, Noizi Ito 2005
First published in Japan in 2005 by KADOKAWA CORPORATION, Tokyo.
English translation rights arranged with KADOKAWA CORPORATION, Tokyo,
through TUTTLE-MORI AGENCY, INC., Tokyo.

English translation © 2011 by Yen Press, LLC

Yen On
150 West 30th Street, 19th Floor
New York, NY 10001

Visit us at yenpress.com
facebook.com/yenpress
twitter.com/yenpress
yenpress.tumblr.com
instagram.com/yenpress

First Yen On Edition: March 2021
Previously published in paperback and hardcover by Yen Press in November 2011.

Yen On is an imprint of Yen Press, LLC.
The Yen On name and logo are trademarks of Yen Press, LLC.

The publisher is not responsible for websites (or their content) that are not owned by the publisher.

The Library of Congress has catalogued the hardcover and previous paperback as follows:
Tanigawa, Nagaru.
[Suzumiya Haruhi no douyou. English]
The wavering of Haruhi Suzumiya / Nagaru Tanigawa ; [English translation by Paul Starr].—1st U.S. ed.
p. cm.
ISBN 978-0-316-03891-1 (hc) / ISBN 978-0-316-03892-8 (pb)
[1. Supernatural—Fiction. 2. Clubs—Fiction. 3. Japan—Fiction.] I. Starr, Paul Tuttle. II. Title.
PZ7.T16139Wav 2011 [Fic]—dc22
2011012965

ISBN: 978-1-9753-2288-5

1 3 5 7 9 10 8 6 4 2

LSC-C

Printed in the United States of America

THE WAVERING
OF HARUHI SUZUMIYA

NAGARU TANIGAWA

First released in Japan in 2003, *The Melancholy of Haruhi Suzumiya* quickly established itself as a publishing phenomenon, drawing much of its inspiration from Japanese pop culture and Japanese comics in particular. With this foundation, the original publication of each book in the Haruhi series included several black-and-white spot illustrations as well as a four-page color insert—all of which are faithfully reproduced here to preserve the authenticity of the first-ever English edition.

CONTENTS

LIVE ALIVE

The year I started high school.

Now that I think about it, a lot happened that year—the year that the meteorological anomaly named Haruhi Suzumiya began to unleash its fury upon North High—in fact, so much happened that trying to remember it all is sort of a pain, and if I really head back into the albums of my memory, the various episodes carved thereon would be enough to make your head spin, if I do say so myself, and yet I'd like to relate one of them now.

The heat of summer continued to coil over the archipelago; the calendar claimed it was autumn, but it was hot enough that I began to harbor suspicions that someone somewhere had thrown a wrench into the works of some terrible weather-control weapon.

It was the day of the school festival.

A certain reliably insane director/producer's mess of a movie, complete with special effects that played havoc with the CHR of the cast and crew, had come all the way from said director's declaration of intent to complete it solely thanks to my efforts. Today was the premiere of *The Adventures of Mikuru Asahina Episode*

00, and though I wasn't sure whether it was a movie or simply a promo reel for Asahina, it was probably being met with rave reviews at the moment in the A/V room.

I say "probably" because, having absolutely no desire to be further associated with a film whose absurdity challenged the borders of surrealism, I'd decided to disassociate myself from it completely after handing over the DV tape to the guys in the film society.

Fortunately, as brigade chief, Haruhi was even more fired up than normal when it came to negotiating the public-relations arrangements, so she had taken the initiative.

While the students and faculty of North High were beginning to get used to Haruhi's activities, it wouldn't have killed her to consider the idle parents and other festivalgoers before donning a certain bunny girl costume from the previous spring, but at least her promotional efforts did allow Asahina, Nagato, and Koizumi to participate in their classes' activities, which, unlike class 1-5 (which included Haruhi and me), actually involved some kind of effort.

Now I felt as though the skies had cleared, and I was as calm as the mirrorlike surface of a serene pool. With the completion of the digital editing of the film, my work was done, and shaking my slightly sleep-deprived head, I had time to maybe walk by Nagato's fortune-telling booth or snicker at Koizumi's play. North High might well have been a shabby public school with a shabby festival to match, but still, a festival was a festival and they didn't happen every day, so it would be nice to enjoy the mood.

Plus, there was one duty I had to fulfill, which took the form of the scrap of paper I had clasped in my hand.

It went without saying that said scrap was a coupon good for a discount at Asahina's class activity—which was a yakisoba café.

When even the cheapest tea became heavenly ambrosia when prepared by Asahina, surely yakisoba prepared by her hand would be finer than the finest Chinese kitchen could prepare—more than enough to raise the anticipation gauge in my mind to stomach-growling levels. As I ascended the school's staircase, it felt more like I was flying up on winged shoes.

But just as I crested the stairs and felt as though heaven's gate lay just before me, the voice of a fellow traveler doused my mood in lukewarm water.

"Man, they could've at least let us eat for free."

Who could be the owner of such an ungrateful tongue? None but my classmate Taniguchi. I had invited him along only out of guilt from the way he'd had to jump into the pond during our location shoot, and he should've been grateful to get that much. What more did he want?

"I had to dive into a pond! And I wasn't getting paid! By the way, nobody invited me to a screening. Don't tell me my scene got cut. Thirty percent off yakisoba ain't enough reward for getting wet like that."

Enough of your grumbling! Asahina went out of her way to give us these coupons. And she was the one who hadn't been fairly compensated for her work in that movie. It was enough to make me want to call up the Academy and get them to give her an Oscar.

"If you don't like it, don't come. Just get lost already," I said.

"Aw, c'mon, Taniguchi. We were just going to wander around and eat stuff anyway, right? We should be thankful for the company," said his companion.

It was another classmate, Kunikida, who had a model-student face that was somehow different from Koizumi's.

He continued. "Plus, if we go with Kyon, we might get something extra. A bigger serving of cabbage, maybe. That'd be worth it, right, Taniguchi?"

"I guess."

Taniguchi readily agreed.

"But that depends on the flavor. Hey, Kyon—Asahina's not doing the actual cooking, is she?"

Now that he mentioned it, I seemed to recall that she'd said she was in charge of table service—but what did it matter? I gave him a questioning look.

"Oh, I was just thinking she's probably a lousy cook. Like, I could imagine her putting in sugar instead of salt or something."

Nobody gave Asahina any credit—not Haruhi, not this guy either. I didn't care how much of a cartoon maid character she looked like; people that clumsy only exist in the realm of the imagination. All she might worry about would be misplacing her time machine and if she really was a time traveler, though even that was doubtful.

"I'm looking forward to it," said Kunikida. "I've been hearing rumors that it's a cosplay café. The waitress costume from the movie and that bunny girl outfit from before were crazy enough, but I wonder what she'll be wearing now."

"Seriously."

Taniguchi nodded heartily—neither of them had grown as accustomed as I had to seeing Asahina in her maid outfit. I had to spare them some pity.

As we crested the stairs and entered the hallway, I imagined the scene. Speaking of waitresses, my brain had already been tainted by the image of her wearing that sexual harassment–inspiring waitress costume in the movie, so what could be better for cleansing both eyes and mind than the sight of her elegantly bringing us our yakisoba wearing a proper waitress outfit? I'd always felt Haruhi's tastes were too gaudy. She had the ironclad nerve to stand at the school entrance dressed as a bunny girl, which might have suited her perfectly, but if she thought everyone possessed such nerve, she was sadly mistaken.

Asahina wearing a waitress uniform handmade for her by her class…

On this matter, I had no choice but to agree with Taniguchi. I was very much looking forward to seeing it. Oh, yes.

Green rubber sheets had been laid down to cover the floor of the school hallways, like some sort of cheap red carpet. Normally, inside shoes were required inside the school, but out of consideration for visitors, outside shoes were allowed for the two days of the festival. There was quite a variety of people walking around too. The art and culture clubs all had presentations set up, and many attendees seemed to be related to the members. The festival was also a place for neighborhood residents to kill some time. It was also pretty common for students to invite their former middle school classmates who'd wound up going to different high schools. This made it the year's only chance to make a pass at the students from the girls' school at the bottom of the hill. It wasn't just guys like Taniguchi who were looking for love.

There in the hall where anything besides a North High uniform would stick out, the three of us forged ahead like sardines swimming toward bait as we navigated the second-year students' classroom displays, finally stopping between the Whac-A-Mole game room and the one doing balloon animals.

The mouthwatering scent of frying wafted out, and there was a sign that proclaimed YAKISOBA CAFÉ ACORN. The line that snaked out of it was longer than for any other classroom. But that wasn't what first jumped out at us.

"Hey! Kyon and his pals! Over here! Welcome, welcome!"

It was a voice and smile totally unmistakable, even from ten meters away. Save Haruhi when she's thought of something annoying, I know only one person who can smile that brightly.

"A table for three, then? Welcome!"

It was Tsuruya—and dressed as a waitress, to boot.

Standing in front of a desk placed outside the classroom entrance, she seemed to be in charge of selling tickets. And probably attracting customers, come to think of it.

"Hey, whaddya think of my getup? Looks pretty schweet, eh?"

Tsuruya moved agilely along the line toward us.

"It sure does."

I kept a pointlessly low profile as I gazed at Tsuruya.

I'd been so occupied with my visions of Waitress Action Asahina that I'd totally forgotten that Tsuruya was in the same class. Taking in the sight of this long-haired upperclassman, Taniguchi and Kunikida looked like fishermen who'd caught a trout, only to find a bass attached to its tail. And who could blame them? I didn't know who'd designed the outfit, but evidently there was a master dressmaker in Tsuruya's class. It had a different look than the outfit Asahina had been made to wear for the movie; neither too gaudy nor too plain, it gave the wearer an elegance without being distracting, working with her natural charm to bring it to a maximum; it deserved a Costume of the Year award, surely.

The point is, the effect was enough to make me resort to abstract terms like this. And if that's what seeing Tsuruya did, a glance at Asahina would no doubt render me immediately unconscious.

"Business looks good," I said.

"Ha ha ha! Yeah, they're really biting!"

Tsuruya lifted the hem of her skirt slightly and, ignoring the glares of the rest of the line, continued.

"It's terrible yakisoba made from the cheapest ingredients, but look at how many people there are! I can't stop laughing!"

Her laugh seemed genuinely happy. It wasn't hard to figure out why the line out the front door was composed entirely of guys. Looking at Tsuruya's smile made even me feel strangely pleasant. I suppose it's true that men are the more easily wiled sex.

We took our place at the end of the line, and Tsuruya directed her smile at us free of charge as she spoke.

"Pay up front, if you please! We've got yakisoba and water on the menu—the noodles are three hundred yen, but you can down all the water you want for free!"

Upon seeing my coupon, she added, "Hmm, so there are three of you, right? We'll say five hundred yen for the lot of you! Big discount!"

She put the coins we gave her in her pocket and then shoved three yakisoba tickets into my hands.

"Alrighty then, just wait a teensy bit! Your turn'll be up in no time!" she said, then returned to her place behind the desk at the classroom's entrance. Once she disappeared at the head of the line, Kunikida spoke.

"She's got energy, that's for sure. You'd think she'd get tired, being like that all the time."

Kunikida sounded impressed as he spoke. Taniguchi lowered his voice and added this:

"Kyon, I've been wondering about this for a while—what's with her? Is she in your and Haruhi's gang or what?"

"Nope."

Tsuruya wasn't in the club. Just like Taniguchi and Kunikida, she's a special guest we bring in when we're short on numbers. And yet somehow, she keeps turning up.

Tsuruya's notion of "no time" turned out to be about half an hour. After waiting for thirty minutes, we finally made it to the front of the line and were allowed to enter the room. Incidentally, the line behind us grew constantly longer, and it was all guys—unbelievable. Though I suppose we could hardly complain. After all, we were in the line too.

Half of the classroom was devoted to cooking, while the other half had tables for seating customers. Several hot plates sizzled away, cooking piles of yakisoba. Some white-aproned girls manned the hot plates, while others chopped away at ingredients with cooking knives, and suddenly I wondered where all the boys in this class had gone.

Later, I heard from Tsuruya that the poor boys had been drafted into running errands for the girls — going to get ingredients they were running low on or fetching water and rinsing vegetables. Alas, there was nothing to be done. The Age of Aquarius was truly nigh.

Tsuruya showed us to our table.

"Okay, just sit right there at that table. Hey! Three waters over here!"

A charming reply came in response to Tsuruya's call.

"Coming right up! Oh, welcome!"

Surely I needn't mention who the perfect waitress was who now came, bearing a tray with three cups of water on it.

After she finished placing the three cups of water on our table, she clasped the tray in both hands and bowed politely.

"Welcome, and thank you for coming to our shop!" she said with a beatific smile. "Kyon, and your, er — the extras from the…"

My two companions reacted instantly.

"Taniguchi!"

"Kunikida!"

"Hee hee. I'm Mikuru Asahina."

I could see why there was a handwritten sign dangling from the ceiling that said PLEASE REFRAIN FROM TAKING PHOTOGRAPHS. If they were to allow pictures, there'd be no avoiding a minor stampede.

That's just how lovely Asahina was. Unsurprisingly, my consciousness went winging away to some far-off place, and surely no more words are necessary to describe her charm. To see her and Tsuruya both wearing the outfit that itself rated a Best Costume Design award, well—it's hard to imagine a finer sight. Heaven must be a place where such views are commonplace.

Asahina held the tray under one arm as she tore the yakisoba tickets in half, leaving the stubs on our table.

"Please wait just a moment," she said.

She hurried back to the kitchen, monopolizing the gazes of all the boys in the room.

Tsuruya smiled and explained.

"Mikuru's taking tickets, clearing plates, and serving water. That's all we let her do! Can't have our main attraction tripping and spilling yakisoba everywhere, after all!"

Wise words, Tsuruya.

A different second-year waitress brought us our food. In exchange for giving extra cabbage, they seemed to have skimped on the meat, and as to whether or not the food was good, well—it tasted like normal yakisoba sauce. Asahina was kept very busy as she jumped robinlike from table to table, putting out paper cups of water and tearing tickets, and it was all she could do to stop by our table once to provide refills of not particularly cold water. Tsuruya shuttled between the classroom and the shop front, smiling all the while, and I felt a bit uncomfortable staying for much longer.

So after finishing our yakisoba in about five minutes, we left, putting the place behind us, though we didn't feel particularly full, nor did we have anywhere else to go.

"So, what next?" It was Kunikida who'd asked. "I kind of want to see the film that Kyon and his friends made. Plus, I need to see how I look in it. What about you, Taniguchi?"

"I've got no interest in seeing that thing," said Taniguchi flatly, taking a festival schedule pamphlet out of his uniform's pocket. "That yakisoba wasn't nearly enough. My plan is to head over to the science club's barbecue party, but before that . . ." He grinned.

"This is a rare and golden opportunity—for picking up some chicks! The trick is to go for girls wearing street clothes. Surely we can spot a group of three all walking together. Chat 'em up a little, and my experience indicates that they're surprisingly likely to go along with whatever you say."

What experience? What good is the experience of a guy whose success rate is just about zero? I shook my head immediately.

"Forget it. You guys go on without me."

"Hmph."

Taniguchi smiled unpleasantly, and Kunikida nodded with a self-satisfied smile, which grated on me, but I couldn't find a retort. It wasn't that I was afraid I'd be spotted by somebody inconvenient if we started hitting on girls, it was just, uh...just because.

"Fine by me. That's just the kind of guy you are. No, don't bother with excuses. I guess that's friendship for you."

Taniguchi sighed dramatically, and Kunikida spoke up to mollify him.

"Actually, Taniguchi—I think I'll pass on the girls too. Sorry, but if you have any luck on your own, could you introduce her friend to me? That's friendship for you, after all," he said, side-stepping the issue. "See you later, okay?"

Kunikida walked briskly away. As Taniguchi stood there staring like an idiot, I decided to follow Kunikida's example.

"See you later, Taniguchi. You can tell me tonight about your success rate—that is, if you succeed at all."

So, where to go next?

If I went back to the clubroom, there'd either be nobody there or I would bump into Haruhi, and if we wound up walking around the school together, no doubt she would do something insane that would destroy my reputation, so my feet naturally took me in another direction. If she had kept conducting her PR campaign at the front gate in that bunny girl outfit, someone might have stopped her by now, and she could well be sulking all alone in the clubroom. Please, just let me do something else today! My mom and sister were coming the next day, and I could just imagine Haruhi crashing the proceedings.

I took another look at the program. There wasn't much of interest. I wasn't interested in the results of the school survey, nor did I have any intention of spending time on ridiculous displays about things like research into the distribution of local dandelion varieties. I'd well and truly had my fill of the kinds of movies each grade seemed to have made one or two of, and I did not care about amateurish art displays or cardboard labyrinths. Was there any point in a handball tournament against other schools' teams? Only our homeroom teacher, Okabe, seemed to be excited about that.

"The best thing for killing time would be…"

My eyes lit upon it. The sole event with any kind of ambition to it—they'd probably been preparing for it more than any other group. Now that I thought about it, I'd recently heard the trumpets blaring away late into the night.

"The orchestra concert it is, then."

I checked the pamphlet again. Unfortunately they wouldn't be performing until the next day. Lots of groups seemed to have signed up to use the auditorium. The drama club and the chorus club were the next day too. Today, the space was booked up by—

"The pop music club and other registered bands, eh?"

It was pretty standard for a school festival, and although it would probably be mostly cover bands, taking in some live music isn't a bad thing once in a while. They had probably put in a hundred times the effort and enthusiasm that I'd put into making that movie. I'll go listen to the results of their labor and just kind of space out, I thought. At the very least, I'd be able to put the terrible film I'd made out of my mind.

"A man needs time to himself sometimes."

So I told myself, having no idea that my notions were about to be blown to smithereens.

I was naive—I thought there were limits in this world. Even though I knew there was a being who could ignore such limits as she pleased, I'd somehow forgotten that. Despite the maelstrom of chaos I'd experienced just a few days previous, I suppose this was what the limits of the common-sense man were. The extraordinary events I was plunged into showed me my own shallowness. I'd like to leave this as a lesson to future generations. Let's not worry about whether or not such lessons would be taken seriously.

The auditorium doors were wide open, and from within boomed a terrific racket, as though the god of thunder had decided to hold a concert. It was a bit cheap as venues for the soul of rock go, but so long as the spirit is there, worrying about issues of technique is like quibbling over condiments on your natto. It's not better without condiments, but the natto is a strong fermented soybean—it's the main event, so to demand it with stuff on it without even tasting it first seems a bit rude.

Perhaps a sixth of the auditorium was full, and most of the people seemed to be the organizers. Onstage, an amateur band did their best with a straight-up cover of a pop song that sounded vaguely familiar. You know it's bad when you can tell they're "doing their best," but the broadcast club's mixing seemed like it might have been part of the problem.

The lights were concentrated on the stage, leaving the rest of the space rather dim. I searched for and found an empty row of chairs and took a seat at the row's edge.

According to the program, the participating groups were the pop music club's band and two other groups. At the moment it was the pop music club performing. Only the people in the very front row of chairs were standing, and while a few of them moved their bodies to the music, I decided they had to be either fellow club members or plants. And anyway, the volume was pumped up way too high for the kind of laid-back listening I had in mind.

I clasped my hands behind my head and watched as, during an interlude of their last number, the vocalist rhythmically introduced the other members of the band, and I learned that they were five second-year pals from the pop music club—information I would surely forget within a few days.

My knowledge of music wasn't deep enough to say anything on the subject, and without any particular interest in the performers, it was the perfect situation for lulling me into complacency.

As a result, I actually started to relax.

And then, as the five members of the current band exited to scattered applause and the next band took the stage—

I couldn't help but rub my eyes in disbelief.

"Guh—"

I could feel the atmosphere of the auditorium change in an instant. The sound of the audience drawing nervously away from the stage became a sound effect that echoed within my head.

"What the hell is that idiot doing?!"

The figure that now walked on from stage left carrying a music stand wore a certain familiar bunny girl costume and a certain familiar expression as she stood there, awash in the stage lighting.

Bunny ears bouncing and figure scantily clad—I could tell you who she was even if you plucked my eyes out and gave them to somebody else.

It was Haruhi Suzumiya.

And she was now standing in the middle of the stage with a serious expression on her face.

And if that had been all, it would've been okay—but no.

"Hnng!"

Upon seeing the figure that appeared behind her, the air in my lungs escaped with a groan.

It was a sometimes evil alien sorceress, sometimes black-clad, crystal ball–wielding fortune-teller.

"..."

I could no longer make a sound.

Yuki Nagato was standing there in that black hat and cape I'd long since gotten sick of seeing, only for some reason she now had a guitar slung over her shoulder. Just what the hell is going on here?

I might have been relieved if Asahina and Koizumi had shown up after that, but the third and fourth people to take the stage were female students I'd never seen before. From their unfamiliar faces and somehow adult aura, I guessed they were third-year students. One had a bass guitar and the other sat down at the drum set. There didn't seem to be any further band members.

Why? I wanted to avert my eyes at the sight of Haruhi and Nagato in their festival costumes. But why—why were they part of a band that was supposed to be made up of members of the pop music club, and why was Haruhi holding the mic like she was the band leader?

As the questions fought each other in my head, all four members of the mysterious group seemed to have taken their places. The audience murmured, and as I looked on, dumbfounded, the bassist and drummer nervously tinkered with their instruments; Nagato did not so much as move to play her guitar. Her face was as expressionless as it usually was.

Haruhi placed what looked like sheet music on the music stand in front of her, then looked slowly over the auditorium. Given the darkness in which the audience sat, I doubted she saw me. Haruhi tapped the mic to make sure it was on, then turned around and said something to the drummer.

There was no introduction and no stage patter. The drummer counted off the beat on her drumsticks, and the band was suddenly playing. The intro alone was enough to blow me away. Nagato's guitar technique was up there with Mark Knopfler's or Brian May's. And I'd never heard the song before. No sooner did I think *What is this?* than Haruhi began singing, as if to deal me a final blow.

Her voice was clear and bright—so clear and so bright it could've reached to the moon.

But her eyes never wavered from the sheet music.

I didn't recover from my stunned state for the entire duration of the first song. I wondered if this was how a monster in an RPG feels when "Silence" has been cast on it.

Onstage, Haruhi was mostly still as she stood there belting out the lyrics, but I guess it's hard to read sheet music and dance at the same time.

The first song wrapped up. Normally that's when the audience would erupt into cheers and applause, but everybody else was just as stunned as I was.

I had no idea how this had happened. It was strange enough to see Haruhi up there, but I was even more amazed by Nagato's melodious guitar technique, and no doubt the other members of the pop music club were filled with the same questions I was. And the people in the audience who didn't know who Haruhi was had to be wondering: Why a bunny girl?

We were frozen like sailors aboard a tattered sailing vessel who'd just heard a siren's song. When I looked more closely, I saw that the bassist and drummer were looking at Nagato and Haruhi with similar expressions. Apparently it wasn't just the audience who'd been stunned.

Haruhi just stood there staring straight ahead, but eventually her brow furrowed and she looked behind her. The drummer, chastened, hastily counted off the next song.

Setting aside the various personages, the mysterious band was now on their third song.

Now that I'd finally gotten over the shock, I could appreciate the lyrics and music I was hearing. It was an up-tempo R&B number. The song was unfamiliar yet pleasant in my ears, and I had to admit it was pretty good. That might have been thanks to the absurdly good guitarist, but Haruhi was, well—how do I put this? Maybe I was too used to hearing her yelling all the time, but I had to admit she had an excellent singing voice.

The rest of the audience, too, seemed to have shaken off its petrification and were now genuinely drawn toward the stage.

When I thought to look around, I realized many more seats had filled up. My eye soon fell on one audience member in particular, who walked toward me wearing what looked like the civilian clothes of a knight of Denmark.

"Hi there," he said, coming in close to speak into my ear, perhaps concerned his voice would be lost in the loud music. "What exactly is going on here?"

It was Koizumi.

How the hell should I know? I shouted back to him in my head, glancing at his costume. You're in a festival getup too, eh?

"Changing clothes seemed like it would be a bit of a bother, so I came in my stage outfit."

And what're you doing here?

Koizumi looked over to Haruhi onstage pleasantly, then flicked his bangs.

"Oh, I just heard some rumors."

So it's a rumor already, eh?

"Oh, yes. She's wearing that outfit, after all, so it would be stranger if there weren't rumors. People do talk."

Evidently, news that North High's prize weirdo, Haruhi Suzumiya, was up to something again was already spreading like wildfire. I didn't care if she added another incident to her reputation, but for once, I didn't want myself or the SOS Brigade getting added to the report.

"But still, she's quite good, Suzumiya is. Nagato too, of course."

Koizumi smiled and closed his eyes as if enjoying the music. I turned my gaze back to the stage and tried to read something, anything, from Haruhi's form.

My opinion of the singing and performance was much the same as Koizumi's, save for the strange fact that the lead singer was reading her performance from sheet music on the music stand.

But all that aside, something nagged at me, something I couldn't put my finger on. What could this ticklish sensation be? I wondered.

The next song was a slow-moving ballad, as if to throw the previous up-tempo song into contrast. I found myself moved by the music and lyrics. It had been some time since a piece of music had pierced my heart like that. As proof that I wasn't the only one who felt that way, the audience was quiet, without so much as a single throat-clearing, and when the song ended, the auditorium fell totally silent.

The room was on its way to being a full house when Haruhi finally spoke into the mic.

"Uh, hello, everybody…"

Haruhi's expression was rigid.

"Here's where we should introduce the band, but the truth is…" She pointed to Nagato. "Nagato and I aren't members. We're just stand-ins. Due to various circumstances, the real vocalist and guitarist couldn't be onstage. Oh, and they're the same person — the real band is just a trio."

The audience listened carefully.

Haruhi moved away from the center of the stage and walked over to the bassist, thrusting the mic at the girl. The girl shied away, whispering something to Haruhi, then finally squeaked out her own name.

Haruhi next walked over to the drum set and got the drummer to introduce herself, then returned to center stage.

"These two and the leader who's not here are the real members. So...sorry. I really don't have any confidence that I'm much of a stand-in. We only had an hour to rehearse before performing, so this is a little off the cuff."

The bunny ears on Haruhi's head flicked as she moved.

"How about this—if you want to hear the songs with the real vocals and guitar, bring a tape or minidisc over later and we'll dub you a copy for free. Is that okay?"

The bassist nodded awkwardly in response to Haruhi's question.

"Okay, it's decided."

Haruhi smiled for the first time since taking the stage. She must have been nervous—or nervous by her standards, anyway—but it seemed the curse was finally broken, and while her smile wasn't as bright as the one she always showed us in the clubroom, it was still a good fifty watts.

After smiling briefly to the still-expressionless Nagato, Haruhi shouted as though to blow out the speaker cones.

"This is the last song!"

I heard the rest of the story from Haruhi later.

"I was handing out movie flyers at the front gate when I ran out, and I was going to head back to the clubroom for more," she said.

"But then there was some kind of argument going on by the shoe lockers between the members of that band and the festival organizers from the student council. I wondered what was up, so I got closer."

As a bunny?

"Who cares what I was wearing? Anyway, from what I gathered, the band wasn't going to be allowed to go onstage."

The shoe lockers are hardly the place for a discussion like that.

"It was because the band leader, who played guitar and sang, had suddenly come down with a fever on the day of the festival. Tonsillitis, I guess. Her voice was mostly gone, and she looked like she could barely stand."

Rotten luck.

"I know. Worse, she'd sprained her wrist after getting dizzy and tripping at home. There was no way she could get on that stage."

So why bother coming to school?

"Yeah, she was determined to do it even if it killed her. But the student council people just wanted to get her to the hospital right away, and she wound up getting carried off like an alien bound for Area Fifty-One. Push came to shove, and they wound up by the shoe lockers."

How did she propose to perform in that condition?

"By sheer willpower."

Sounds like something you'd do.

"I mean, they'd practiced so hard for this day. It's one thing if she were the only one who was going to suffer if it went to waste — but wasting the efforts of your friends too? That's awful."

You make it sound like it was your own efforts.

"And the songs too — they weren't generic cover songs, but originals the group had written and composed themselves. You've just got to perform them, right? If the sheet music could talk, it'd say, 'Play me!'"

So that's when you decided to roll up your sleeves and do something about it.

"Didn't have any sleeves, but yeah. The student council festival committee is nothing but a bunch of incompetents who do whatever the teachers tell them, so you can't just let them push you around. But... even I knew there was no way the band leader was going onstage in her condition. So that's when I said, 'How about I go onstage instead?'"

I can't believe the bassist and drummer went along with it.

"The singing part was easy. The sick band leader thought about it for a second and then said, 'Yeah, you might be able to do it.' She had a tired-looking smile."

There isn't a North High student who doesn't know who Haruhi is, and what kind of girl.

"But then a teacher had to hurry off to the hospital with the band leader, and I started frantically trying to learn the chords from a demo tape and the sheet music. I only had an hour, after all."

So what about Nagato?

"Yeah, I wish I could've played the guitar too, but there just wasn't enough time. It was all I could do to learn the melody, so I wound up asking Yuki to handle the guitar. Did you know she was such an all-around player?"

As a matter of fact, I do know that—better than you do.

"I crashed her fortune-telling stall, and when I told her the circumstances, she came right away. She just took one look at the sheet music, then played it perfectly! Where do you think she learned guitar?"

Probably right on the spot, as soon as you asked her to.

A couple of days later, on the following Monday—

The school festival, complete with its unscheduled events, had ended. It was the break before fourth period.

Haruhi sat behind me, happily scribbling something down in her notebook. I didn't particularly want to know what it was, but I knew Haruhi was pleased by the audience the SOS Brigade's foray into independent filmmaking had managed to reach, and she seemed to be plunging into the planning of the sequel as I agonized over how to banish such notions from her head.

"You've got visitors."

It was Kunikida who'd said so, having returned from the bathroom.

"For Suzumiya," he added.

Haruhi looked up and saw Kunikida point to the doorway, thus fulfilling his duties as a messenger boy. He returned to his seat.

Three female students stood outside the open door, poised and mature. One of them had her arm in a sling.

"Haruhi," I said.

I gestured with my chin toward the door.

"Looks like they have something to say to you. Better go see."

"Mmm."

Haruhi seemed strangely hesitant. She stood slowly but did not immediately walk. Finally she wound up saying this:

"Kyon, you come too."

Before I could protest, she grabbed me by the collar and hauled me with her absurd strength right out of the classroom. The three upperclassmen girls giggled at the sight.

Haruhi forced me to stand right next to her.

"Is your tonsillitis better?" she asked the one girl, whom I was just now meeting for the first time.

"Yes, mostly," she answered in a voice that was just slightly husky. "Thank you, Suzumiya."

All three girls bowed deeply in gratitude.

It turned out that practically the whole school (especially the girls) had requested copies of their songs. They said they were now going around to all the classes and distributing minidiscs.

"I can't believe how many requests there were."

When I heard the figure, I was surprised myself. There'd been quite a ripple effect indeed if people were going to such lengths to get the original songs instead of the one with Haruhi on vocals and Nagato on guitar.

"And it's all thanks to you."

All three girls had the same grateful smile for their helpful younger classmate.

"This means our songs won't have gone to waste. We really appreciate it. You're something else, Suzumiya. This was going to be our last memory as members of the pop music club, so I wanted to go onstage if I could, but this was way better than missing out entirely. We just can't thank you enough."

It felt a little embarrassing to have three seniors being so grateful, and I wasn't even the one being thanked. Why do I have to stand here and be embarrassed along with Haruhi?

"We were hoping we could do something for you in return," said the leader, but Haruhi waved her off.

"Don't worry about it! It was fun for me to sing, and the songs were good, so it was like getting to do karaoke with a live band for free—you don't need to thank me, really. I'd feel bad."

Something about Haruhi's tone was odd, as though she'd prepared the speech ahead of time—although it was very like her to speak so casually to upperclassmen.

"So really, don't bother. If you want to thank someone, thank Yuki. I forced her into doing it, after all."

The girls explained that they'd already been by Nagato's class.

Evidently, after listening to the girls' words of gratitude, the stoic Nagato had nodded once, then pointed to this classroom. I had no trouble imagining it.

"Well then," said the leader. "We're going to try to have a concert somewhere before graduation, so you should come if you want. With your…"

She looked at me and narrowed her eyes just slightly.

"…friend."

But why had there been such demand for the girls' original recording?

I'd found this out later. You can't really call it a mystery, but in any case it had been solved by a certain talkative fellow. He does come in handy, I'll admit.

"Did you notice any discrepancy between the timing of Suzumiya and that of the rhythm section? Or more properly, between the melody Suzumiya was singing, Nagato's riffs, and the bass and drums?" asked Koizumi.

"It was only noticeable on a subconscious level. All four of them were playing together so well, you'd never guess they were winging it. What's most surprising is Suzumiya's ear. Keep in mind she'd only heard the demo tape three times."

I wanted to be impressed with Nagato's professional-level playing as well, but the fact is that kind of thing is easy for her.

"Yet it wasn't perfect. Those *were* original songs, after all. There's simply a huge difference between the performers who wrote those songs and practiced them endlessly and Suzumiya, who performed as an emergency stand-in."

Well, obviously.

"Yes. So between the original bassist and drummer, Suzumiya's idiosyncratic performance of songs she rushed to learn, and Nagato's guitar following those idiosyncrasies, there were discrepancies—tiny, but they were there. And as the audience listened, they would feel the tension, if only subconsciously."

He was being as plausible as he always was. Do you think anything is possible with enough psychobabble?

"It's what I concluded after my analysis. Moving along, then— when they played the second and third songs, the feeling of tension only increased, and then they reached the final song. And what did Suzumiya do then?"

She'd explained that the real guitarist and vocalist weren't onstage, that she and Nagato were just stand-ins, and then she introduced the drummer and bassist...right?

"And that was enough. In that instant, the mystery was solved— the reason for the strange tension in everybody's chest. 'So that's where that strange uncertainty came from,' they thought."

When he put it that way...it did make a certain sense.

"Suzumiya's singing and Nagato's guitar works were by no means bad; far from it, they were well beyond the pop music club's level, but the audience probably thought about it like this: 'If they were this good with stand-in vocals and guitar, they must be amazing with the real leader.'"

So that explained why there were so many requests for mini-disc copies.

"Suzumiya's singing was excellent, almost perfect. But in not being *too* perfect, she created the best possible outcome. I must say, I'm impressed."

He might have been right. Haruhi popping up had certainly turned out well for those three girls.

So what about us?

"To which 'us' do you refer?"

I'm talking about the SOS Brigade—you know, the people more involved with Haruhi than anyone else at the school! Do you seriously think there's something good waiting for us too?

"I suppose we won't know that until the very end. If we don't think things went too badly once it's all over, I'd say you could call that 'something good.'"

The three older girls left just as the bell announcing fourth period began to ring.

Bafflingly, Haruhi returned to her seat with a complex expression on her face, and it stayed there as she daydreamed straight through the period. She disappeared from the classroom as soon as lunch started.

I wolfed down my lunch as I listened to Kunikida and Taniguchi make their excuses ("Yeah, man, there just weren't any decent chicks at the festival. It's this school's crappy location, I'm telling you—it needs to be on flat ground."), then shoved my lunch box into my school bag and vacated my seat.

For no particular reason, I just felt like taking a walk to digest.

After wandering around for a while, my feet brought me to the courtyard in the middle of the school. I veered off the path that would take me to the clubroom building and walked the patchy, balding lawn in the center. And there, who should I happen across but Haruhi, lying there on the grass.

"Yo," I said. "What's up? You've been wearing that expression since the last recess."

"What of it?"

Haruhi had replied quickly, staring at the clouds as though she were talking to the sky. I did likewise—that is, I looked up at the sky, saying nothing.

I wonder how long we stayed that way, quiet. It didn't feel like more than three minutes, but I don't have a lot of confidence in my internal clock.

It was Haruhi who finally broke the pointless silence contest. Her tone was somehow stiff, reluctant.

"I just can't seem to calm down. I wonder why."

Her tone seemed genuinely puzzled. I felt a sardonic smile coming on.

"How should I know?" I said. Here's what I really wanted to say to her:

It's because you're not used to people thanking you. You're always doing things that no normal person would look you in the eye and say "thank you" for. You were probably secretly wondering if you were butting in when you offered to help them out. If it'd been you, you would've dragged yourself onstage even if your vocal cords were blown out or both your arms broken. The people around you telling you to stop would only have given you more energy, and you'd never have thought to turn to anybody else for help.

So how does it feel to have helped out those girls? Their songs are hits thanks to you arguing with the festival committee people. When they thanked you, they really meant it. It was almost

the best thing you could've done. So how does it feel, Haruhi? Has this awakened you to the possibilities of good deeds? How about swearing to work only for the good of the world and humanity henceforth?

...Of course I never said any of that stuff. I only thought it. All I was doing was standing next to Haruhi and looking up at the sky. A mountain breeze blew thin clouds through the sky, as though the school festival itself had triggered the autumn weather.

Haruhi said nothing. She wore an intentional-looking scowl on her face, but within her head was probably another emotion entirely.

"What?" Haruhi directed an annoyed glare at me but remained where she was. "You got something to say? Then say it. I'm sure it's nothing worthwhile, but it's bad to just stew on things."

Her eyes glittered.

"Not really, no," I said.

Haruhi sat up and grabbed a handful of grass to throw at me. But evidently the weather gods were on my side, as a sudden odd gust of wind blew up and set the green blades back into her face.

"Ugh!"

Haruhi flopped back down on the grass as she sputtered to get the grass out of her mouth.

I looked vaguely up at the clubroom building. I could see the brigade room's window from here. I wondered if a certain slender, short-haired figure would be looking down at us, but there was nobody there. Not surprising, I guessed.

The silence continued for a bit longer but was eventually broken by Haruhi's voice.

"Concerts are fun. I sort of wonder if that was good enough, but...yeah. It was fun. How should I put it? It felt like I was really doing something."

If dressing as a bunny girl and getting up onstage to sing lyrics from a music stand as a substitute vocalist was her idea of fun, then she had serious guts. Of course, I knew that already.

"I can see why that injured girl argued so much with the festival committee," she said.

"Yeah."

I couldn't help but feel sort of moved. I guess that's what I get for letting my guard down.

"Hey!"

The tranquil mood was shattered when Haruhi suddenly bolted to her feet, then loomed over me ominously. I tried to back away, but my foot slipped.

The volatile Haruhi smiled brilliantly and spoke in a high, excited voice.

"Hey, Kyon! Can you play an instrument?"

"Nope."

I shook my head rapidly. I had a very bad feeling about this.

"Huh. Well, we'll fix that with practice. We've got a whole year, after all."

Hey, now.

"We should perform as a band next year! We don't have to join the pop music club if we pass the audition, and that'll be a cinch. I'll do vocals, Yuki can play guitar, and we'll give Mikuru a tambourine and put her onstage as decoration!"

Oh hell no.

"Of course, we've got to make the sequel to the movie too. We're gonna be busy next year—but you always gotta set more goals, right?"

Now hang on just a second!

"All right, Kyon, let's go!"

Hey, wait—go where, to do what?

"To get some instruments! They'll have some spares in the pop music club room. And I'll have to ask those three girls about tips for writing songs. Gotta strike while the iron's hot!"

Haruhi ignored me as I considered how hesitating before striking was probably the best idea. She grabbed my wrist and began to drag me behind her.

Her strides were long. Purposeful.

"Don't worry; I'll handle the songwriting and composition. And the arrangement and choreography, of course."

Oh, great. The mysterious switch in Haruhi's head had been flipped, and she was off on some new obsession. Even alien abductors would drag me off more gently than she did. I looked up at the sky for someone to help me.

No one was standing at the clubroom window. Apparently our own genius-level guitarist/magic-wielding alien was absorbed in a book right now. It was autumn, after all.

"C'mon, Kyon, walk with your own two feet. Three stairs at a leap, got it?"

Haruhi turned and looked back, eyes glittering with all she was imagining, and she lengthened her stride into a run.

There was no helping it. I ran too.

Why, you ask?

Because it would be some time before Haruhi let go of my hand.

Thus did my first school festival come to a hurried end, as though linked with the changing season—though the festival's energy seemed to echo in Haruhi's mind, and behind that echo danced boldly typeset headline copy like, "Pre-Sale Tickets Now Being Designed!" or "(Hopefully) A Smash Hit in the US!" or "A Year to Plan, A Month to Shoot (More or Less)."

She was already thinking about the sequel she wanted to make for next year's festival. You might think that no one would be so hasty—but you'd be wrong.

For my part, I felt like I'd just managed to finish delivering a heavy package, and just as I was feeling like I could go home, suddenly I had to deliver an even heavier load. I was escorting the terrified leading lady down a treacherous jungle path, waiting to be ambushed by a Bengal tiger, the two of us quivering in fear, all because of that insane thing we'd just screened.

How insane? Read on, my friend.

THE ADVENTURES OF MIKURU ASAHINA EPISODE 00

Her name was Mikuru Asahina, and while she seemed to be a normal, healthy, attractive lass, she was actually a time traveler from the future. I'd like to assure you that any relationship to a person you might already know named Mikuru Asahina is purely coincidental.

Moving along. The truth about Mikuru Asahina is that she was a combat waitress from the future. Why did a waitress have to travel back in time? And why did she have to dress up as a waitress? Such matters are no more than trivialities and, to be quite frank, are meaningless. Any explanation beyond "that is simply the way things are" is impossible, and in fact, none of the individuals here can lay claim to a meaningful raison d'être.

... A booming voice from the heavens has simply declared it to be so.

So, then, let us observe the life of this Mikuru Asahina.

Normally, she was dressed as a bunny girl, as her daily routine involved attracting customers to a neighborhood grocery store. In the evenings, she put on her bunny girl costume and, holding a signboard there in front of the store, she called out the specials in her lovely voice—in other words, she held down a part-time job.

Because she came all the way from the future, you might think she would have a more effective means of supporting herself, but this story was created without any consideration for notions like "realism," and I thought it would be kindest to make that clear, so that you didn't set your expectations too high.

So, we have here a combat waitress from the future who also dresses as a bunny girl.

I'll say up front that you will never find out just why it is that she wears such outfits. It is meaningless. And even if there were some meaning, it would surely never be revealed, which is effectively the same as being meaningless.

Today, as usual, Mikuru Asahina had cheerfully donned her bunny girl outfit and was eking out her living, signboard in hand.

"Sorry to trouble you during your busy day! There's a new shipment of fresh cabbage today! And for a limited time, for the next hour, each head of cabbage will be half price! Excuse me, madam—please try some!"

There she was, stiffly raising her voice in front of the grocer's. The bunny ears atop her head aren't the only thing that bounces and jiggles with the movements of her petite frame, and while you would think the housewives that make up most of the store's clientele wouldn't be enticed by such charm, Mikuru's earnestness brought smiles from all around her, and such smiles helped open wallets.

"You're always so energetic, Mikuru," said a passerby stiffly, as though reading from a script.

Mikuru smiled her fluorescent-pink sunflower smile. "Th-thank you! I'm doing my best!" she replied brightly, her innocent charm shining out into the shopping district.

Then she spoke again, her words a spell with the magical ability to transform a household's menu from whatever had been planned into cabbage stew.

"Supplies are limited! Get them while they last!"

The grocery store was immediately swarmed, and soon every last head of cabbage had been sold.

Mikuru was then called into the rear of the store by the manager, Mr. Kiyosumi Morimura (age forty-six), who gave her an envelope containing her day's pay.

"Thank you again. This isn't much, but please take it."

Mr. Morimura's wrinkled, careworn face was lowered as Mikuru accepted the money from his strong hand.

"Oh, not at all. I'm the one who should thank you. This is all I can do, after all…"

Mikuru, being a faithfully polite girl, bowed deeply. She then tucked the envelope into her ample bosom.

"Well then, if you'll excuse me, I must be off to the butcher's. Good-bye!"

Carrying her signboard, Mikuru trotted off through the shopping district. Truly, she had become an irreplaceable mascot for the district, beloved by all.

Best of luck to you, Mikuru! Take back the customers stolen by the giant store that opened last year! The revitalization of the local mom-and-pop stores rests on your shoulders!

One can't help but want to shout such exhortations to her.

However, Mikuru did not travel back in time just to rescue a declining shopping district from ruin. Her bunny outfit was a cover; we mustn't forget that her true identity was that of a combat waitress. It really doesn't matter either way, but that's the way it is, and there's nothing to be done about it.

So, then—Mikuru's true purpose, her mission, was to secretly protect a certain young man.

That young man's name was none other than Itsuki Koizumi, who might seem like a completely ordinary high school student, but who was actually an esper. I'm sure it goes without saying that any resemblance this person might bear to anybody else named Itsuki Koizumi is entirely coincidental.

Now, although he was an esper, Itsuki Koizumi himself was unaware of that fact. Evidently it would take some sort of trigger to awaken the supernatural power within him, but for now, that power lay dormant for his own safety, and from both a subjective and an objective perspective, his life was no different from an ordinary high school student's.

Today, like any other day, Itsuki Koizumi wore his backpack and a carefree smile as he walked home from school. His path took him right down the main street of this shopping district.

"..."

A shadowy figure secretly watched Itsuki's receding form. From the two long ears that protruded from the figure's head and its nearly-naked-seeming silhouette, even a fool could tell it was Mikuru. You might wonder why she would be stealthily following someone while wearing that outfit, but keep in mind it was her usual clothing, and thus could hardly be helped.

"Whew."

Mikuru sighed, apparently relieved that Itsuki seemed to be safe. Her sigh also seemed like the sound a younger student would make while gazing longingly at the dreamy upperclassman she has a crush on, but such thoughts are infuriating, so we'll ignore this latter possibility.

After watching Itsuki go, Mikuru took her sign, complete with *Beef Skirt, 98 Yen/100g (heart symbol, original drawing of a cow)* written in Magic Marker on it, and walked in the opposite direction from Itsuki's, heading to her next job, looking a bit dejected as she went.

Having nodded in response to the many greetings that were directed at her on the way, she finally arrived at her destination, which was a dim little stationery shop. The shopkeeper, one Mr. Yusuke Suzuki (age sixty-five), was the head of the local merchants' council, and he furnished Mikuru with her current lodgings.

"Welcome back, Mikuru. Are you tired?"

Mr. Suzuki greeted Mikuru with a kindly smile, though his intonation was strangely wooden.

"Um, I'm fine. There were lots of customers, and...business was...um, what was it...oh yes, booming."

"Well, that's good."

Mikuru gave Mr. Suzuki a bow, then climbed the shop's steep stairs to get to her room. At the end of the short hallway was her residence in this time period: a small Japanese-style bedroom.

Mr. Suzuki lived elsewhere, so this room had been vacant. I'm not sure exactly what the process had been, but in any case, Mikuru had come to live here after arriving from the future.

After sliding the door to the room closed, Mikuru began to take off her bunny girl outfit. Unfortunately, this scene was cut. In the next scene, she wore a baggy T-shirt as she climbed into her futon—then that scene, too, ended.

Meanwhile, another pair of eyes gazed thoughtfully upon Itsuki Koizumi.

They belonged to a girl named Yuki Nagato. She hardly looked like a normal schoolgirl, and small wonder, for she was actually an evil alien sorceress. You could easily guess as much, for she wore a cape and a wide-brimmed pointed hat—both well outside modern clothing standards. Incidentally, any resemblance she bears to anyone else named Yuki Nagato is completely coincidental, and this explanation is starting to get really old.

"…"

Yuki stood upon the rooftop of the school, her face not betraying a single emotion. This was the school that Itsuki attended, and although this was no doubt intended as a scene to show that she also had some sort of intention toward him, given the sequence of events, Itsuki had long since gone home, leaving Yuki standing there atop the unoccupied school, making the cut to this scene difficult to understand.

The previous scene was shot around sunset, yet from the position of the sun in the southern sky above Yuki's head, it now seemed to be the height of midday, which unambiguously led to the conclusion that this scene had been shot during a lunch break. One can imagine how the director's insistence on filming with a total disregard for logical sequence must have given the editor endless headaches.

That trend held true for the subsequent narrative.

Because of time constraints, Mikuru and Yuki entered their first confrontation without so much as a single explanation for why this might be happening.

After Mikuru ran pointlessly through a flock of pigeons at a shrine, the scene shifted to what seemed to be a forested park.

She, of course, was no longer dressed as a bunny girl, but instead as a waitress whose skirt was far too short. Mikuru, her hair tied up in pigtails and wearing an outfit that did amazing things for her assets, gripped a heavy-looking automatic pistol in each hand. Her face wore a sympathy-inspiring expression of tremulous resignation—and this was not an expression she'd been told to assume, but rather a reflection of her true feelings.

Meanwhile, the black-clad Yuki Nagato betrayed no emotion at all; she just stood there, motionless, holding a magic wand tipped with a star.

The two girls faced each other. It was no doubt intended to be a deadly face-off, but the encounter was too tame to be called as much, perhaps because Mikuru seemed to have nervously judged her own chances of winning such an encounter to be rather slim.

"Yah!"

Mikuru squeezed her eyes shut and aimed her guns blindly as she pulled the triggers in rapid succession. The small pellets came shooting out of the barrels toward Yuki, though most of them went well wide of her, and you could count the shots that were actually aimed properly on the fingers of one hand.

Naturally, Mikuru's enemy would not simply sit there while she was attacked. With her left hand she waved Star Ring Inferno, her absurdly named magic wand, and deflected the shots.

"Oh no…"

Shortly, Mikuru was out of ammunition, and silence fell.

"I-I guess I'll have to use my last resort! Take that!"

Although it felt a little too early to be using one's last resort, Mikuru gave a shout with her charming little voice and opened her eyes wide.

Her hand came up, fingers forming a horizontal V shape around her bright blue left eye.

"M-M-Mikuru Beam!" she cried out, and from her eye shot a deadly laser beam. The death ray would burn through the air at the speed of light, piercing anything in its path—or it would have, but there was someone who would not let that happen.

Yuki Nagato.

Teleporting without the use of trick editing, Yuki reached out and blocked the Mikuru Beam with her right hand. Before the natural-sounding *hiss* of the beam could be heard, Yuki lunged toward Mikuru.

"Eek—!"

Mikuru cowered before the black form that rushed toward her. Yuki moved toward Mikuru with such speed that her black cloak billowed out, and she grabbed Mikuru's face and tackled her to the ground.

"Yaah! N-Nagato, wha—!"

The battle waitress flailed her limbs as Yuki sat on her.

What could possibly happen next? What will Mikuru's fate be? Why is Itsuki here?

All these questions will be answered after this message from Omori Electronics, delivered by our two leading ladies.

Our story resumes after the commercial, as Waitress Mikuru walks dejectedly along.

"I can't believe the Mikuru Beam didn't work...I've got to do something!"

She muttered to herself as she trudged through the shopping district. Her clothing in disarray, Mikuru arrived at the stationery shop where she lived, and closing herself up in her bare, unfurnished room, she changed clothes again. Evidently she was not a transforming magical girl and had to change outfits like everybody else.

The sliding door to her room opened, and Mikuru emerged, once again wearing her bunny girl costume. Downcast, she descended the stairs.

Evidently, regardless of the outcome of her battle, she had to work again today. Whether she's honest or just foolish—or simply a hard worker—she was certainly enduring a lot of hardship, which was not far from the experiences of the actress.

Incidentally, at that moment, Itsuki Koizumi was walking down the street with a vacant expression on his face.

Before him appeared that elusive black-clad figure, Yuki Nagato. Yuki now had a calico cat riding on her shoulder, which hung on by digging its claws into her cloak. It seemed more worried about

keeping its balance than Yuki was. Unobtrusive as ever, her appearance in Itsuki's path was quite sudden.

Itsuki looked surprised as he stopped in front of the cat-carrying sorceress.

"What are you?"

A more appropriate reaction might have been nicer, but in any case that is what he said.

"I am—"

Yuki paused.

"—an alien sorceress."

Looking at the cat, Itsuki replied:

"Is that so?"

"It is."

Yuki also looked at the cat.

"What do you want with me?"

"You have a hidden power, which I am after."

"And what if I say it's too much trouble?"

"I will have you, even if I must use force."

"What kind of force do you mean?"

"This."

Yuki waved the Star Ring Inferno. Immediately, a thunderbolt leaped from the star atop the wand.

"Look out!"

A bunny girl tackled Itsuki from the side, and the two toppled over, limbs tangled. The thunderbolt went wide, splitting a telephone pole.

Itsuki was collapsed atop Bunny Mikuru—a deeply infuriating sight. For some reason, Yuki did not press her attack.

Perhaps it was that Mikuru seemed to be stunned after hitting her head in the fall. Itsuki shook her by the shoulders, and she seemed to come around.

"Owww…"

Mikuru stood as she rubbed her head, then pointed resolutely at Yuki, then called out.

"I won't let you do as you please!"

Yuki looked first at Mikuru, then expressionlessly at the whiskers of the cat on her shoulder, before returning her gaze to the battle waitress and speaking quietly.

"I will retreat for the time being, but this will not happen again. Use what time is left to you to prepare your gravestone, for next time I shall show you no mercy," said Yuki as she turned to leave, although there was no reason for her to show Mikuru any mercy now either.

Itsuki spoke.

"Who are you?"

"Huh —?" said Mikuru, who was suddenly tense after having begun to look relieved. "Um, er... I'm just a passing bunny girl! Never mind me! Um, good-bye!"

She ran off after Yuki.

"Whoever could she be?" said Itsuki, eyes gazing pointlessly into the distance as the camera panned just as pointlessly up at the white clouds in the sky.

The next round of "Mikuru versus Yuki" took place by a pond.

It went without saying that the details regarding why they had come to this particular place were entirely omitted. Apparently some things happened, and their conflict had been reignited, or whatever.

"I-I-I'm not going to back down, e-e-evil alien Yuki! L-leave Earth at once! Um... I'm sorry..."

"It is you who should disappear from this time period. He belongs to us. He has value to us. Though he has not realized his own power, it is critical. We will use that power to invade Earth."

"I w-w-won't let that happen! Not on my l-l-life!"

"Very well. I will take that life."

Yuki did not have her cat with her this time. Instead, she had three other companions, who from their uniforms appeared to be high school students—an energetic-looking girl and two puzzled boys.

Mikuru seemed to know the long-haired girl, at least.

"Oh, um, Tsuruya! Not…not you too! Come b-back to your senses!"

"How am I supposed to come to any senses at all with you dressed like that?"

Tsuruya replied immediately, her acting slipping for just a moment. She curled her lip maliciously and continued.

"Sorry, Mikuru. I don't want to do this, but I'm being controlled. Sorry, really!"

"Eek!"

"Now prepare yourself!"

Tsuruya and the two others approached Mikuru in an entirely nonthreatening fashion.

Behind them, Yuki waved her wand as though giving commands. Whether it was psychic emissions or electromagnetic radiation, something seemed to be emanating from the wand and robbing Tsuruya and the two others of their volition, turning them into puppets to be controlled.

Yuki Nagato was a force to be reckoned with. Such a cowardly attack! How could Mikuru fight back against this? Mikuru, whatever shall you do?

"Eek! Eeeee—!"

Nothing, apparently.

The pitiful girl found herself grabbed by the arms and legs by Tsuruya and the two boys and tossed into the brackish green water of the pond. One of the boys—the more clownish-looking one—seemed to stumble, and he took a dive from the edge of the pond as well. Not that it mattered. He'd probably haul himself out.

"Eek! Blug…gah!"

Evidently the pond was deep enough that Mikuru's feet didn't reach the bottom. Panicked, she beat at the water frantically, but in her urgency she was hardly making any progress at all. Before long, she'd be fish food. She couldn't swim—or at least, she'd been told she couldn't swim, so all she could do was flail in the water. Mikuru Asahina was in a pinch.

But there was someone who could save our heroine.

"What happened?"

Along came the dashing, gallant Itsuki Koizumi to the rescue. Kneeling down at the edge of the pond, he extended his hand to the convincingly drowning Mikuru in a manner that can only be described as "comic-book-like."

"Grab hold—but be careful. Don't pull me in with you."

Just where had Itsuki been all this time? The pond was surrounded by flat ground—there was nowhere to hide, and yet from his timing, he must have been watching all along. Even more strangely, the wand-waving Yuki, along with her three zombified flunkies, had disappeared. She had been on the cusp of victory—where had she gone?

"Are you all right?"

"…Oooh…So cold…"

After being dragged out by Itsuki, Mikuru coughed, crawling on all fours.

"What were you doing in a place like that?" asked Itsuki.

Mikuru did not immediately answer, simply staring blankly at him, but eventually she seemed to remember her line.

"Um, uh…some bad people, they…um…"

A voice sounded from offscreen, and Mikuru suddenly moaned and collapsed. Yes, the script says she faints.

"Get a hold of yourself!"

Itsuki tried to pick up Mikuru, but she went limp in his arms.

Normally at times like these, you would think the person in

Itsuki's role would call an ambulance or get help from a bystander, but Itsuki—that cad!—just lifted Mikuru onto his back and started walking off somewhere. *Just where in the hell are you taking that beautiful, helpless girl?* you might want to call out, but his stride did not waver.

He walked off, as purposefully as though he himself was being remotely controlled by mind-altering waves.

But to where?

To a house, it turned out. His.

Despite the omission of scene-setting details, based on the spacious, traditional-style bedroom Itsuki laid Mikuru down in, we can infer that his house is a large one indeed, and built in the Japanese style.

Notably, Itsuki had committed the outrage of carrying the now-T-shirt-clad Mikuru in his arms, and Mikuru looked unavoidably as though she had just bathed.

As it's quite impossible to imagine just how an unconscious person is supposed to be able to bathe themselves, doubts cannot help but surface in one's mind about what else this scoundrel may have done to her while his hands were washing her body, and such doubts would immediately turn to rage, which in turn might become murderous intent—and there's that murderous intent, right on schedule.

Itsuki should be less worried about Yuki and more worried about how he's going to protect himself from half the school's student population.

Taking an unconscious, half-drowned girl to his own bedroom was crime enough, but to give her a bath transcended mere criminality and was a fundamentally evil act, and there could be no complaint upon the summary execution of the person—Itsuki—responsible. Please, someone punish this man.

In any case, Itsuki placed Mikuru on a futon that had suddenly

appeared, then sat down cross-legged beside her. He folded his arms and appeared to be deep in thought. But I'd wager he wasn't thinking a damned thing. Any takers?

As proof, upon hearing directions from someone offscreen, he leaned over Mikuru. If that bastard Koizumi—I mean, Itsuki—had moved so much as one centimeter farther, someone who wasn't supposed to be there was going to have to break the fourth wall and kick the crap out of him, but fortunately he was interrupted by someone else, whose appearance was less surprising.

"Wait."

It was Yuki Nagato, coming in through the window and looking like some kind of half-baked grim reaper's apprentice. I forgot to mention that this was on the second floor. That may lead you to wonder where she was standing this entire time. Please just suspend your disbelief.

Yuki—who was maybe more of a black-clad angel in mourning than a pseudo-reaper—clambered through the window, then stood.

"Itsuki Koizumi. You should not choose her. Your power will only become effective at my side."

Yuki spoke flatly, regarding Itsuki with dark, ever-calm eyes.

Itsuki being Itsuki, he showed no alarm at a girl climbing into his room through a second-story window.

"Huh? What do you mean by that?"

His reply was awfully straight, his face serious.

"I cannot explain now. But you will understand soon enough. You have two choices. You can join me and help advance the universe toward its ideal form, or you may side with her and snuff out the possibilities of the future."

As I recall, perhaps a third of this line was ad-libbed by Yuki. Was it really meant only for Itsuki, I wonder?

We'll set aside for a moment the implication of Nagato's—I

mean, Yuki's—words. Itsuki's face looked troubled as he contemplated.

"I see. So either way, he…or, in this scene, it would be me, I am the key, am I not? And the key itself has no power. At best, a key can only open a door. When that door is opened, something will change. The thing that will change is…"

Itsuki paused for a moment and for some reason looked directly at the camera. Just who the hell was he looking at, and what the hell was he trying to say?

"I understand, Yuki. But as I am now, I do not have the right to decide. I think it is too early to draw any conclusions. Shall we table this matter, then? We still need time to consider. Of course, if you're willing to divulge everything, then that's a different matter."

"That time will come soon. But it is not yet upon us, that is certain. We customarily view a lack of information as a flaw. We do not act without certainty."

It was an opaque conversation, but there seemed to be a kind of incomprehensible understanding developing between Itsuki and Yuki.

Yuki nodded slowly, and after glancing at Mikuru's flushed face, clambered out the window and disappeared. She didn't fall from the second floor, though; she was just standing on the eaves, but in any case, you couldn't see her anymore.

Itsuki resumed his thoughtful expression and looked back at the sleeping Mikuru.

When Mikuru awakes, will she comprehend the particulars of her situation and, enraged, throw whatever's handy at Itsuki? All alone with a boy, unconscious, wearing nothing but a T-shirt—it's not unreasonable that she'd conclude that something had happened to her and blame Itsuki, right? I'd like very much for that to happen.

But instead of fulfilling any such expectations, it's time for another commercial break. Please enjoy our two leading ladies delivering a promotion for Yamachi Model Shop.

...

After the commercial, the story hit a turning point. The combat-themed plot thus far was completely and inexplicably eclipsed by a romantic comedy.

Mikuru seemed to have moved in with Itsuki, and the resulting cheesy cohabitation story was so terrible you want to pass out rather than endure the embarrassment of watching it anymore.

Here was Mikuru cheerfully offering Itsuki her terrible cooking, and there she was blushing furiously and making a big fuss over accidentally brushing his finger while seeing him off to school from the house's front door, and now she was doing the cleaning and laundry, and finally she happily greeted Itsuki as he arrived home from school.

It was enough to make me want to scream, "Oh God, please stop this," but such pleas were likely to fall upon deaf ears, as Itsuki and Mikuru's touching love story dragged on for an eternity. Hey, Koizumi—want to trade places?

Incidentally, Itsuki Koizumi lived with his younger sister, it turned out, so a ten-year-old fifth grader was hauled in—sorry, her birthday was last month, so I guess she was eleven. Anyway, now she was fooling around with Itsuki and Mikuru on-screen in yet another scene that makes the fate of the story quite a mystery. What was the point of giving Itsuki a sister, anyway?

Amidst all of this, the incomprehensible battle between Mikuru and Yuki over Itsuki's fate had now moved to Itsuki's school.

Shockingly, Yuki transferred to Itsuki's high school. Why we're using such sluggish filler material, I have no idea, but in any event, Yuki abandoned her black robes and pursued a more indirect method of pursuing her target, cleverly attempting to push Mikuru aside while becoming closer to Itsuki. She left no psychological attack untested—she left love letters in his shoe locker, brought two box lunches and forced one on him at lunchtime, staked out the front gate and intercepted him as he left school, secretly took photos of him and kept them in her wallet, and so on and so on. That all seemed more like a frontal assault than a clever scheme, though.

Of course, Mikuru struck back. She also transferred into Itsuki's school. Wouldn't it have made more sense to just have her there to begin with? If her raison d'être is protecting Itsuki, it wouldn't have been strange for her to be in school with him—on the contrary, it would've made more sense that way.

Without any explanation whatsoever, for some mysterious reason Mikuru and Yuki never fought with laser beams and magic spells on school grounds. Apparently their goal had become trying to be the first to capture Itsuki's heart.

The story went completely off the rails, devolving into a narrative about two girls vying for the affections of one boy.

Of course, Yuki had a huge problem. After all, Mikuru lived under the same roof as Itsuki, giving her an advantage that was like the Great Wall of China, making Yuki (where did she live, anyway?) an invading Hun, totally unable to get over the barrier.

To make a comeback, Yuki would have to resort to extreme methods.

"…"

"Hey, what are you doing?"

Yuki started hugging Itsuki regardless of time and place. No doubt the sudden feminine physical contact was meant to leave Itsuki shaken, but Yuki's face was so expressionless, it's hard to ascertain what, if anything, she was feeling, and it was more eerie and off-putting than anything else.

Her facial expression had no relationship to her actions.

Although Mikuru managed to act jealous every time she saw

the two of them, from outside Itsuki appeared not to care one way or the other, so there was no real emotion conveyed at all.

It was as though it didn't really matter what happened to Itsuki.

And owing to time constraints, it was about time to gather everybody together for one last gasp at the finale.

Perhaps because they were bored with the lighthearted school scenes and the cease-fire that applied on the school grounds, or perhaps because their true identities simply came through sometimes, Mikuru and Yuki now resumed their original roles of Battle Waitress and Alien Sorcerer and skirmished sporadically.

With each scene, the depth of the plot's confusion increased as it progressed thusly:

—Mikuru fighting Yuki and Yuki's cat familiar, Shamisen, in an apartment complex courtyard.

—Mikuru and Yuki (with Shamisen) tossing firecrackers at each other in the bamboo forest behind the school.

—Mikuru and Yuki wrestling each other in front of some unknown person's house, with a bored Shamisen looking on.

—Mikuru and Yuki chasing each other around Itsuki's living room, while Itsuki's little sister holds Shamisen and laughs.

And just when you think we've made it through these pointless scenes, the film flirted with exhaustion yet again as it dredged up the school/love-triangle plot.

Itsuki thus far had remained indecisive on the matter of Mikuru and Yuki, which of course would earn him cries of resentment from all around him—from the other boys, that is. But the Ultra Director who ruled this story like a god chucked all such complaints out of the ring and obstinately imposed her own will.

Which would explain why the story so far had careened out of control, like a chimpanzee playing a racing game, crashing at every corner then rampaging ahead anyway.

But even the Ultra Director eventually realized that despite the play-it-by-ear philosophy she'd used thus far, if she didn't wrap things up soon, they'd never get to the ending at all.

Of course, it was already too late, if you asked me.

Anyway, perhaps she realized that at this rate there'd be no story at all, so all the little scenes with the characters doing who-knows-what got forcibly mashed together as we rushed toward the end.

Yuki suddenly remembered her original purpose and informed Mikuru of their final confrontation.

One morning, Mikuru opened her shoe locker to find a note reading LET'S FINISH THIS in mechanically written letters that looked like some printer had spit them out.

But still—if Yuki had really wanted to take out Mikuru, she'd had scores of opportunities thus far, and she wouldn't have had to go to the trouble of informing Mikuru ahead of time. And yet who can fathom the mind of a space alien who goes around pretending to be a normal, expressionless high school student while constantly battling with her opponent? What did she want, anyway?

And who had any idea what Mikuru wanted either? After reading the missive from Yuki, she looked off into space with a steely gaze, gripping the note and nodding decisively as though having realized something. What had she realized? I know I've said this before, but I had no idea. The only one who knows won't ever be on-screen.

As for me, behind the camera, well, comprehension was impossible, but thankfully I knew that everything in this world comes to an end eventually, giving salvation from this eternal hell.

We had arrived at the climax.

Appearing again for another cameo, Tsuruya came up to the troubled-looking Mikuru.

"What's the matter, Mikuru? You look like you're worried about some old man stalking you. Did your doctor tell you that you have athlete's foot or something?"

Crouching in the corner of the classroom, Mikuru replied.

"The time has finally come. I must go and face the final battle!"

"Wow, how 'bout that! I'll leave you to it, then—Earth's in your hands!"

Tsuruya kept a straight face when she delivered the line, but then her face twitched and she burst out laughing.

"...I'll do my best..."

Mikuru's reply was so soft that the mic could barely pick it up.

Incidentally, although it's probably pointless to point out any more problems with this terrible story, just when did Mikuru become friends with Tsuruya? Tsuruya's first appearance was as a mind-controlled puppet in the pond scene, and Mikuru seemed to already know her at that point, which means that she knew Tsuruya even before Mikuru transferred into this school. But if that's the case, Yuki's mind-control attack should have happened later. At the very least, the knowledge that Tsuruya and Mikuru were friends would have improved that scene, and the fact that it didn't play out that way is frankly a mistake.

Of course, the voice of God believed herself to be infallible, and she had no time for such observations, instead pouring all her energy into immediately filming whatever scene popped into her head. With no idea of when her instinct-driven activities might cease, ordinary humans like me were run totally ragged in both mind and body.

Thus did the final battle come to be held on the school rooftop.

During the lunch hour, the black-robed Yuki waited with Shamisen draped over her shoulder.

After a few seconds, the doors to the roof opened and out came Mikuru, dressed in her combat waitress outfit.

"D-did I keep you waiting?"

"Yes."

Yuki answered honestly. Mikuru had needed to change in a stall in the girls' bathroom, and while I didn't know whether that was why she had taken so long, she'd kept the cameraman waiting for quite a while too.

"Well then," said Yuki.

Her honesty was dispensed with, and she now launched into the lines that had been prepared for her.

"Let us settle this now. We do not have much time. We must end this in a few minutes, at the most."

"I agree, but…but! Itsuki will definitely choose me! Um… this is embarrassing, but I believe it's true!"

"Unfortunately, I do not plan to respect his wishes. I require his power, and I will have it. If I must, I will conquer Earth to get it."

Why couldn't she just go ahead and conquer Earth, and then gain control of Itsuki after she'd done so? No one would be able to resist her then, and Mikuru would be left to struggle alone as the majority went ahead and handed over Itsuki—not even the loveliest of battle waitresses would be able to stop them.

And anyway, if she had the power to conquer Earth, shouldn't capturing just one person be no problem?

"I won't let you! That's why I've come from the future!"

Oh, right. Mikuru was a waitress from the future. That fact had been used hardly at all so far, so I was starting to wonder.

The laser-beam fight scenes between Yuki and Mikuru now started again.

On one hand, you had Mikuru firing beams, trip lines, missiles, and micro black holes while shouting "Shazam!" and "Kapow!" and so on, while Yuki wordlessly waved her wand around.

The word of God came down that there were some effects you just couldn't do with CG, so a variety of firecrackers were set off atop the school, and although they were old castoffs from the shopping district's toy store, they were still plenty loud when lit. The resulting racket attracted the attention of several teachers down below, and we all got an earful.

That's what happens when you play with fire at school, obviously.

If anything bad was going to go on my permanent record as a result, I'd ask that it instead be attributed to the director. But even if she shouldered Asahina's, Nagato's, and Koizumi's burdens as well, she'd still be able to get by without any problems, thanks to her excellent grades. If she'd just sit down and shut up, nobody would have any complaints about her.

Despite the cameraman's internal monologue, the battle raged on.

This is thanks to the director's stubborn assertion that if the teachers forced us to withdraw from the rooftop and abandon this important scene, she would file a claim against the school for trying to stifle students' freedom of expression.

I was afraid she'd actually do it too.

The teachers retreated from the rooftop with an impotent request to please not play with fire on school grounds, and we were getting more and more of an audience coming up through the roof's entrance, which made Mikuru even more nervous.

One thing led to another, and Mikuru wound up at the end of her rope. None of her attacks had affected Yuki, and as she'd backed away from the constantly advancing alien sorcerer, she was cornered against the roof's railing.

"Be at peace. I will carve you a fine epitaph. Be sure and do many good deeds in the afterlife, so as to store up good karma for your next life." Yuki delivered her parting words as she thrust her wand at the waitress. "Farewell."

That instant, the Star Ring Whatever lit up absurdly, and there was a cheap flashing effect that flickered several times.

"Eeeeek!"

Mikuru clutched her head and collapsed into a fetal position.

It wasn't clear what kind of attack Yuki used, but evidently it was very powerful. It may have looked as though it was only causing the screen to flicker, but it was a spell potent enough to disintegrate Mikuru right down to the last atom.

If you don't get excited here, there's not going to be any more opportunities for excitement, so thanks in advance.

"Eeeek! Aaaaah!"

Mikuru continued to cry out.

It would be easy to get annoyed at such a totally useless heroine, but she was so cute that all was forgiven.

And even forgiven, she was at this rate about to be erased from the story. If evil triumphed over good, the narrative would become an ironic commentary on the fact that no matter the predominant views on who should succeed, those with power would always win.

"..."

But of course, that is not what happened. The character who stood on the side of justice right up through the very end was not suddenly going to disappear. The hand of an unseen god would move to exterminate evil, allowing a crucial character to appear with unbelievably exquisite timing. That was the scenario the director had dreamed up.

It goes without saying that the deus ex machina that saved Mikuru was none other than Itsuki Koizumi. I mean, of course. Who else would it be? There wasn't enough time to suddenly introduce another character, after all.

In a flash, Itsuki picked Mikuru up, successfully dodging Yuki's assault. It was awfully slow, that magical ray of Yuki's.

"Asahina, are you all right?" said Itsuki, who then turned to face Yuki, holding out his arm. "I cannot allow you to hurt her. Yuki, please stop this."

Seeing Itsuki's determined stance in front of the helpless Mikuru, Yuki looked at the cat on her shoulder as if contemplating something. Perhaps she was considering annihilating them both, if she indeed could not have Itsuki.

But the answer came from an unexpected source.

"There is nothing to consider. You have only to steal the boy's will. From what I've heard, you have the ability to control others. Simply take control of him, then, and hide him away somewhere, then deal with the girl at your leisure."

Shamisen spoke, and I freaked out. I'd told him not to speak, so what the hell was he doing? No dinner for him!

"Understood."

Yuki, composed as always, bopped Shamisen on the forehead with the star that tipped her wand. The cat shut his mouth. Yuki then spoke again, to nobody in particular.

"That was ventriloquism."

She then raised the Star Whatever.

"Take this, Itsuki Koizumi. Your will becomes mine."

A cheap special-effect thunderbolt leaped from the star.

I'm sure it's obvious what happened next, but I suppose I might as well relate the events of the last battle.

To make a long story short, Itsuki's potential power was realized. Having found himself in a desperate situation, he activated the latent potency that he never knew he had and his full abilities were unleashed. Such powers are often difficult to control, and Itsuki's case was no different. The force of his emotion caused his incomprehensible power to reflect Yuki's attack back on her with incredible energy.

"...How unfortunate."

"Meeooow—!"

And with that, the mysterious Yuki and Shamisen were blown off into the horizon, leaving behind terribly disappointing final words.

Itsuki watched their demise, then spoke to Mikuru in a soft voice.

"It's over, Asahina."

Mikuru looked up tremulously, gazing at Itsuki as though he were a very bright light.

Itsuki put his arm around Mikuru and helped her to her feet, then rested his hand on the roof's guardrail and looked up to the sky. Mikuru followed his gaze to the clouds as the camera panned up.

It was obvious that the camera panned up any time the connection to the next scene was unclear.

Which brought us to the very last scene.

Despite its being autumn, Mikuru and Itsuki walked along a cherry-blossom-filled road. The degree to which her waitress outfit and his school uniform went together is strangely irritating.

Conveniently, a sudden gust of wind arose, sweeping up the scattered petals into little whirls. This was the only natural scene in the film.

Itsuki smiled as he plucked a cherry petal from Mikuru's hair. Mikuru blushed bashfully and slowly closed her eyes.

The camera's focus blurred, then tilted up to capture the blue autumn sky. The sky again? Really?

The intro to the ending theme we stole from somewhere began to play as the credits scrolled.

The voice of God, evidently recorded separately, began to deliver some narration as *The Adventures of Mikuru Asahina Episode 00* came to its conclusion just as confusingly as it began.

Calling a movie filled with such ridiculousness from beginning to end a "movie" is an insult to people who are actually serious about making movies, and yet somehow this wound up being rather popular. The film was supposed to be bookended by features created by the film society, but in the end the audience demand for our film wound up pushing the others aside and monopolizing the film society's projector, no doubt because the voice of God had been hard at work hyping the movie, and also because Mikuru Asahina was quite popular.

Evidently the poor film society ended up screening their movies in little spurts whenever the A/V room was free.

Since we weren't collecting ticket fees, no one was making any money, but the popularity went directly to the director/producer's head, and she immediately proposed a sequel, along with a new edit entitled *The Adventures of Mikuru Asahina: The Director's Cut* that would be burned to DVD and sold, ideas that both myself and a teary-eyed Asahina are trying our best to dissuade her from.

Right now, we're just praying that our brigade chief will turn her antennae toward something besides filmmaking for the next school festival.

But try as we might, no matter what she does, the same fate surely awaits, and that's assuming the SOS Brigade still even exists by that point.

…Will it? I wondered.

I decided I should ask the time traveler. I quietly hoped the information wasn't classified.

LOVE AT FIRST SIGHT

It all began with a phone call.

Just like every other year, the festive Christmas spirit had vanished as soon as the date had passed, and as we counted down the last few days until the new year, for which Haruhi would no doubt have all sorts of plans, I was afforded a few days of peace.

At the time, I had postponed all the house cleaning that needed to be finished before the new year and was instead wrestling with Shamisen in my room.

"Quit struggling! Just hold still; it'll be over in a second!"

"Meow—"

Ignoring his protests, I held the tiny predator with his newly grown winter coat under my arm.

Ever since he'd turned my favorite denim jacket into scrap, my human-average memory suggested I should take the lesson to heart, and I made sure to regularly trim his claws. Shamisen's feline-average memory was good enough, however, that he would sprint desperately away whenever he saw me holding the clippers.

Catching him was a terrible hassle, and holding down the

scratching, kicking, biting calico while I trimmed each of his claws to a reasonable length meant that by the time I was finished, both of my hands were covered in countless scratches. But flesh wounds would heal, unlike the embroidery on my denim jacket, so I had to stay vigilant. It made me long for the days when he could understand and use human speech. You were so cooperative then, Shamisen—what happened?

But if he started talking again, that was an ill omen of another sort, so perhaps it was better if he just meowed like a normal cat.

Just as I was finishing his right paw and moving on to his left—

"Kyon! Phone for you!"

My younger sister burst into the room, holding the cordless phone. She grinned as she saw the struggle for dignity currently taking place between human and feline.

"Oh, Shami! Are you getting your nails clipped? I'll do it!"

Shamisen looked away as if to say "No thanks," sniffing in a very humanlike way. I'd let my sister clip his claws once. I'd held him down while she did the clipping, but an eleven-year-old fifth grader doesn't have much sense for clipping nails, and she'd cut Shamisen's to the quick, annoying him enough to put him off his feed. While I was definitely preferable to her, he still fought me every time. I guess a cat's brain isn't very big, in the end.

"Who is it?"

I traded the nail clippers for the telephone receiver. Shamisen saw his chance and twisted free, pushing off my knee and dashing out of the room.

Holding the nail clippers happily, my sister answered.

"Um, a boy. I don't know who he is. But he said he was your friend."

With that, she ran out into the hallway in pursuit of Shamisen. I looked at the phone.

Who could it be? If it was a boy, that ruled out Haruhi and Asahina, and if it was Koizumi, my sister would've recognized him. My other friends, like Taniguchi or Kunikida, would've called my cell phone, not my home landline. I punched the talk button on the receiver, muttering that I wasn't going to fall for any stupid surveys or sales scams.

"Hello?"

"Hey, Kyon! It's me! Long time no talk!"

I furrowed my brow at the throaty voice.

Who the hell is this? I couldn't pretend I had any recollection of the voice.

"It's me, man! We were in the same class in junior high, remember? Did you forget already? I've been sighing over you for months!"

Now that was downright creepy.

"Tell me your name," I said. "Who *are* you?"

"Nakagawa! Can't you at least remember the name of a classmate from a year ago? Or what, you go to a different high school and suddenly you don't care about your old pals? C'mon, man!"

He sounded genuinely wounded.

"No, that's not it."

I cracked the lid on my memories and thought back to my third year of junior high. Nakagawa, huh? I did remember him. He was a well-built, broad-shouldered guy—I thought he was in the rugby club or something.

And yet...I looked at the receiver again.

We had only been in class together that one year, and we hadn't been close. We hung out in different groups in the class. Sure, we'd say "Hey" or "'Sup" when we passed in the hallway, but if you wanted to know whether we talked every day, I could tell you for sure that we didn't. Since graduation, I hadn't had a single reason to think of his name or face.

I started picking up the claw clippings Shamisen had left behind as I spoke.

"Nakagawa, eh? Yeah, Nakagawa. I guess it has been a while. So, how've you been? I hear you went to an all-boys school somewhere, right? So why are you calling me? Are you working for the alumni association or something?"

"No, the alumni group's headed up by Sudo—he goes to a public high school. But that's not important. I've got something to tell you, okay? So listen. I'm serious."

So what was so serious about this phone call out of the blue? I couldn't possibly imagine what he could be getting at.

"Kyon, you gotta hear me out. This is something I can only tell you. You're my only lifeline here."

Sounds like a bit of an exaggeration. But what the heck, I thought, let's hear him out—let's hear what this estranged former classmate has gone to the trouble of calling me to say.

"It's love."

"..."

"I'm serious. It's killing me. These last few months, it's all I can think about, whether I'm awake or asleep."

"..."

"It's gotten so bad that I can't do anything else. Well, no, that's not true. I've been throwing myself into schoolwork and club activities, just to distract myself. My grades have gone up, and I'm on the varsity team after just a year."

"..."

"And it's all because of love. Do you understand me, Kyon? Do you understand the suffering in my chest? Once I'd looked up your home phone number in the junior high registry, do you know how many times I hesitated to call you? My body's shaking right now. It's love. The incredible power of love has forced me to call you. Please understand."

"Look, Nakagawa..."

I licked my dry lips. A bead of cold sweat dripped down my temple. This was bad.

"...I'm sorry, but your love or whatever is just too...um...all I can say is that I'm sorry. I just can't return your feelings."

A cold shiver ran down my spine, if ever one had. I should say right now that I am 100 percent heterosexual. I don't have a hummingbird's weight worth of desire to bat for the other team. Both potentially and unconsciously, I am totally straight. I mean, consider this—it warms my whole body to think of Asahina's face and figure. But when I think of Koizumi, I just want to sock him. Which means I'm not even bi, right? Right?

I spoke into the receiver without a clear idea of whom I wanted to address my thoughts to.

"So, uh, Nakagawa—we can stay friends, but..."

Not that we had ever been friends to begin with.

"...there's just no way it can be a romantic thing. I'm sorry. Okay? Good luck at that boys' school you're going to. I'm just going to enjoy my normal high school life at North High. It's been good talking to you after so long, though. If we meet at a reunion, don't worry—I won't out you. So, see ya—"

"Wait, Kyon."

Nakagawa sounded suspicious.

"What are you talking about? You've got the wrong idea. I'm not in love with you. What the heck are you thinking? Get your mind out of the gutter!"

So what was that "It's love" thing all about earlier? Whom had those words been meant for?

"I don't actually know her name. I do know she's a student at North High, though."

Although I had no idea what he was going on about, I breathed a sigh of relief. I felt like a foot soldier in a foxhole at the front line of battle who'd just heard news of a treaty being signed. Getting a love confession from a guy was kind of surprising. In my case, anyway.

"Well, then explain yourself better! Who're you in love with?"

There was a limit to how vague you could be, after all. I was just about ready to put him on my block list.

And anyway, what was the big idea, talking so seriously about love while still in his first year of high school? Maybe that was the craziest thing. It was embarrassing just to say it. I mean, love?

"It was this past spring...around May."

Nakagawa started talking. There was something euphoric about his tone.

"She was walking with you. I can still see it clearly every time I close my eyes. Ah, her form was so fetching, so beautiful. And that wasn't all. I saw a radiance shining out from behind her. It was no illusion—yes, it was light as though from heaven itself..."

His rapturous tone had a dangerous edge to it, as though he were under the influence of a dangerous drug.

"I was overwhelmed. I'd never felt such a feeling in my entire life. It was like electricity—no, like a thunderbolt had struck me where I stood! I stood there for hours, having lost all track of time. When I came to my senses, it was nighttime. That's when I knew—it was love."

"Now wait just a minute—"

Nakagawa's words were like the feverish ramblings of an *Andromeda Strain* patient, but I tried to make sense of them. According to him, he'd seen me walking with someone in May, and the sight of that person had overwhelmed him. She was a North High student...which meant there weren't many possibilities.

I hadn't walked around town with many girls this past spring, to be honest. If she was a North High student, that eliminated my sister, so it had to be one of the three girls in the SOS Brigade. Which meant...

"It was a fated encounter."

Nakagawa continued his intoxicated rambling.

"Do you understand, Kyon? I never believed in anything as superstitious as 'love at first sight.' I was a strict materialist. But my eyes have been opened. There is love at first sight—there is, Kyon."

Why did I have to listen to him go on and on about it? Love at first sight? I asked if he was sure he wasn't being deceived by outward appearances.

"No, I'm not."

His reply was decisive.

"I'm not being fooled by either face or figure. It's the inside that's important. I saw through to her soul in an instant. A glance was all it took. Nothing can change the impact it made on me. Unfortunately, it's hard to put into words. But I've fallen in love—I feel like I want to keep falling. Do you understand, Kyon?"

Now it was my turn to say no.

"Forget about that, anyway—" I decided to cut off Nakagawa's inane chatter.

"So you were shocked or whatever by that girl in May, right? But it's winter now. It's been months, so what have you been doing all this time?"

"That's right, Kyon. Now that you mention it, it's been rough. These past few months have been pure suffering. My mind hasn't had a moment's rest. I'm constantly agonizing over what to do. I wonder about what part of me could possibly be worthy of a girl like her. I'll be frank, Kyon. It was only recently that I realized you were the one walking next to her. That's why I called you. That's just how dazzling she is. I've never felt this way about anything else in my life."

The fact that he'd fallen head over heels for a girl whose name he didn't even know, then mooned over her for months was a little frightening.

Asahina's, Haruhi's, and Nagato's faces appeared in my mind; I decided to cut to the chase. To be honest, I just wanted to hang up, but judging by his crazed tone, if I hung up on him he'd just keep redialing me.

"Tell me what the girl you fell for looks like."

After a moment of silence, Nakagawa spoke.

"She had short hair," he said, speaking slowly as he recalled her. "And she wore glasses."

Aha.

"The North High uniform looked spectacular on her."

Uh-huh.

"And she was surrounded by a glittering aura."

Well, I don't know about that.

"So, you're talking about Nagato, then."

This was a surprise. I thought for sure the person he was so crazy for would be either Asahina or Haruhi, but Nagato? I guess there was something to Taniguchi's A-minus grading. My first impression of her had been that she was an antique doll of a girl, quiet and eccentric, but I guess there are girl-connoisseurs everywhere. Of course, now it's different—my opinion of her has completely changed in the last six months.

"So her name's Nagato, then?"

Nakagawa's voice was strangely aroused.

"What characters does she use to write it? What's her full name?"

"Yuki Nagato. Nagato as in the battleship, Yuki as in 'hope,'" I told him.

"...What a lovely name. Her family name is magnificent and strong, like the *Nagato,* while her given name is pure and clear, full of optimism and the possibilities of the future. It's neither banal nor overstated, just like the image of her in my mind."

And just what image was that? How could a single look reflect anything but his own conceited delusion?

"You said it was what was inside that counted, but what does love at first sight have to do with that?" I asked him.

"I just knew."

He was annoyingly confident.

"This isn't just a delusion. I know it. I don't care about outward appearance or personality. It's her intellect. I saw her. She had a godlike intelligence to her. I'll never meet such a highbrow girl again."

There was still much I didn't understand; I'd have to look up "highbrow" in the dictionary later.

"So how can you tell all that from a single glance? You only saw her from a distance, and you haven't said one word to her."

"I can't help it—I just know it's true!"

Why does he have to yell?

"I'm grateful to God. I'm ashamed I never believed in religion before. Now I go to the neighborhood shrine every week to pray, and I've been going to the church for confession—both Protestant and Catholic."

"That just makes you more of an unbeliever," I said. "You can't just worship anything. Pick a god and stick with it!"

"You've got a point," said Nakagawa. "Thank you, Kyon. I've made up my mind. I need worship but one goddess—and that's Yuki Nagato. I'll devote all my life's love to her—"

"Nakagawa."

He'd just keep going with his nonsense if I let him, so I cut him off—it was just too corny, and I was starting to get irritated.

"So what do you want? I get why you called, but what of it? What's the point of declaring your love for Nagato to me?"

"I want you to give her a message for me."

So said Nakagawa.

"I want you to convey to her my words. Please. You're my only hope. You were walking right beside her. Surely you must know her well."

He wasn't wrong. Everyone in the SOS Brigade was in the same orbit around Haruhi. And he'd said he saw Nagato and me in May, and she'd been wearing glasses along with her school uniform. So it must have been the day the SOS Brigade had gone on its first patrol, when I'd gone to the library with her. I got a little nostalgic thinking about it, but compared to then, I know a hundred times more about Nagato now—more than I'd like, if I'm honest.

Feeling it a bit keenly, I put a question to Nakagawa.

"So you remembered that I was walking with Nagato..."

It was a little hard to say.

"So, um, did it occur to you that we might not just be friends? That we might, like, be dating?"

"Not even a little bit," answered Nakagawa without a moment's hesitation. "You're into stranger girls. Like back in junior high... I forget what her name was, but you're not still going out with that one girl?"

There was plenty wrong with the idea that Nagato herself wasn't weird, but that was beside the point—this guy seemed to have the wrong idea. I remembered Kunikida being similarly mistaken. That girl was just a friend, and I hadn't seen her since graduating junior high. This was the first time I'd thought of her in a while. I considered whether I should send her a New Year's card.

I started to feel like I was just digging myself in deeper, so I changed the subject.

"So, what do you want me to tell her? You want to ask her out? Do you just want me to give you her number?"

"No."

Nakagawa's response was serious.

"As I am now, I am not worthy to show my face before her. There's just too much disparity. So that's why—"

He paused for effect.

"—I want you to tell her to wait."

"To wait for what?" I asked.

"To wait for me to come for her. Don't you see? Right now, I'm just a high school student with no value in society at all."

Sure, I thought, but I'm the same way.

"So it's just no good. Listen, Kyon. I'm going to throw myself into study, starting now. No—I already have. I'll go straight into a national university."

It was good to have goals.

"I'm going to study economics. I'll keep working hard, and when I graduate I'll be at the top of my class. And when I start looking for jobs, I'm not going to go into a government or corporate job, but a smaller company instead."

He was laying out a blueprint with no idea whether it was realistic or just a pipe dream. If a demon overheard him, he'd probably die laughing.

"But I won't be satisfied with being a member of the proletariat for long. In three years—no, two years—I'll have gotten the expertise I need to start my own business."

Nobody's going to stop you, so go right ahead, I thought. If I haven't gotten my act together by then, I'd want him to hire me.

"I'll get my company moving in five...no, make that three years, getting listed in the second section of the Tokyo Stock Exchange, with yearly profit growth of at least ten percent—and that's gross profit, I mean."

His spiel was getting harder to follow. But, undaunted, he continued.

"By that time, I'll be able to take a breath. My preparations will be ready, you see."

"What preparations?"

"My preparations to receive Nagato."

I was as silent as a deep-sea shellfish as Nakagawa's words battered me like ocean waves.

"Two years until I graduate from high school, and four years in college. Then two years of on-the-job training, followed by the three years it'll take me to open my company and get it publicly traded, so that's eleven years total. No, let's round it out to an even ten. In ten years I'll be a worthwhile member of society, so—"

"Are you completely stupid?"

I think you'll understand why I said this. What girl would possibly just sit there and wait for a decade? And for a guy she'd never even met? To be asked to wait for ten years for some guy she'd never even met to come and propose to her, and then just sit there and do it, well—no human could do that. Unfortunately, Nagato wasn't human.

I clicked my tongue.

"I'm serious."

He really sounded serious too.

"I'll stake my life on it. I mean it."

If words could cut, his were slicing right through the telephone wires.

How was I going to talk him out of it?

"Listen, Nakagawa..."

I thought about Nagato's slender form as she sat alone, reading.

"...This is just my perspective, but Nagato's actually pretty popular with the guys. It's kind of a problem for her, really. You've got a pretty good eye for girls, I'll say that. But the chance that Nagato's gonna stay single for ten years is about zero."

It was a total bluff. I didn't have a clue what would happen in ten years—not even to myself.

"And besides, something this important should be told to her in person. I'm not wild about it, but I'll introduce you. It's winter vacation, so I'm sure she can spare an hour or so."

"I can't do it."

Nakagawa's voice was suddenly quiet.

"I can't do it right now. I'd faint as soon as I saw her face. Actually, I caught a glimpse of her from a distance the other day. It was at the supermarket by the train station...and I just happened to see her from behind, and that was all it took to freeze me in my tracks. Meeting her in person, I just...I couldn't do it!"

Man, his brain had a bad case of love fever. It was serious, too, if he'd already made his ten-year plan under its influence. I wish there was something to do, but the only cure would be hearing her say "I'm sorry" as she ran away from him on the day he finally worked up the strength to blurt it out.

But if he was so far gone as to tell all this stuff to a guy he barely knew over the phone, I was terrified of what he might say next. I already had one person like that to worry about—Haruhi—and now Nagato had gone and made the problem worse.

What a pain. I sighed loud enough that he'd be able to hear it.

"Fine. Just tell me again what you want me to say to her."

"Thank you, Kyon."

Nakagawa sounded genuinely grateful.

"We'll definitely invite you to the wedding. I'll ask you to give a speech—the first speech too. I'll never forget you. If you want, there will always be a position for you at the company I'm going to start."

"Whatever, just tell me what you want me to say."

I listened to the excessively hasty Nakagawa while balancing the receiver on my shoulder as I looked around for a piece of loose-leaf paper to write on.

Just after noon the next day, I silently walked up the hill to North High. As the elevation rose, the white vapor of my breath became more visible. If you want to know why I was going to school in the middle of vacation, it's because the SOS Brigade was holding its regular meeting.

Today we'd also be doing a thorough cleaning of the clubroom. Although Asahina the maid would diligently sweep the floor, in accordance with the law that says that entropy always increases, a constant influx of stuff coming into the room had disrupted its order. The main sources of this chaos were Haruhi, who would swipe anything that her eye fell upon; Koizumi, who kept bringing in new board games; Nagato, who was constantly tearing through thick books; and Asahina, who was devoted to brewing the perfect cup of tea—basically, everybody but me. Left alone, the clubroom would turn into a disaster area. I'd finally proposed that everyone should take their stuff back to their homes, although Asahina's costume rack would be spared.

"Ugh, what a pain."

It went without saying that the lack of spring in my step was due to the unwanted piece of paper in my blazer pocket.

I'd written down Nakagawa's declaration of love for Nagato verbatim. It was so ridiculous that I'd wanted to chuck my pencil across the room any number of times. Only veteran seducers would be able to say such absurd things with a straight face. "Wait ten years for me?" What was this, some kind of joke?

As I walked into the breeze coming off the hill, the familiar school grounds came into view.

I arrived at the clubroom building an hour ahead of the time Haruhi had set for the meeting.

It wasn't because of the SOS Brigade rule that the last person to arrive for a meeting had to treat everyone else. That rule applied only to after-school activities.

The previous day, Nakagawa had said this:

"You can't just hand over the note. You'd just be a notetaker, then. She might not even read it. You've got to read it out loud in front of her, and with the same passion I just used in telling it to you."

It was an unreasonable request. I had no reason, nor was I simpleton enough, to just do as he said, but I was just enough of a believer in the goodness of humanity to be slightly moved by his entreaties. So to do it, I needed to get Nagato alone, with nobody else around. If I showed up an hour early, I was sure nobody besides Nagato would be there, and Nagato would definitely be there—she was the most reliable alien-built android I knew, after all.

After a perfunctory knock on the door was met by silence, I opened it.

"Hey."

Did that sound too forced? I scolded myself and tried again.

"Hey, Nagato. I figured you'd be here."

There in the tranquil midwinter air that filled the room, Nagato sat quietly in a chair, as still and cold as though she were a life-size doll. The title of the book she was reading sounded like the name of a disease.

"..."

She regarded me expressionlessly, raising her hand to her temple briefly, then lowering it.

It was the same movement she would have used to adjust her glasses, except she didn't wear them anymore. I was the one who'd told her she looked better without them, and she was the one who'd left them off. So what was that just now? Had her habit from a few months ago returned?

"Nobody else is here yet?"

"Not yet."

Nagato answered concisely, then returned her gaze to the densely typeset pages of her book. I wondered if she considered blank spots a waste of space.

I awkwardly made my way toward the window, letting my eyes drift from the clubroom building down to the courtyard below. It was winter vacation, and there was hardly anybody on campus. All I could hear through the drafty window was the faint chanting of one of the more cold-resistant sports clubs.

Standing there, I turned to face Nagato. She looked the way she always did—the same porcelain features and lack of expression.

Now that I thought about it, we'd been short a glasses girl for some time. Haruhi would probably make a play to fill the spot again sooner or later.

I thought about such pointless things as I fumbled for the folded piece of loose-leaf in my pocket, then pulled it out.

"Nagato, there's something I need to tell you."

"What is it?"

Nagato moved a finger to turn a page. I took a deep breath.

"There's this idiot who's obsessed with you, and as his agent I'm going to tell you what he told me. So how about it? Will you listen?"

If she said no, I'd planned to tear up the paper and throw it away right on the spot, but Nagato looked silently up at me. Despite the icy color of her eyes, when they looked at me they seemed to have a warmth that could melt snow—had my explanation been that good?

"..."

Nagato stared at me, her lips closed. Her gaze was like a surgeon peering at a patient.

"I see," she said, watching me unflinchingly. She seemed to be waiting for me, so I helplessly unfolded the paper with Nakagawa's confession on it and started to read.

"My Dearest Miss Yuki Nagato, though I could not help myself, please forgive me for conveying my thoughts to you in this way. In truth, from the very first day I saw you—"

Nagato looked at me and listened. It was I who felt weirder and weirder as I read. The more I spat out Nakagawa's declaration of love, the dizzier I felt, as the stupidity of it all reached a crescendo. What was I doing? Was I crazy?

The final stage of Nakagawa's life plan, as I read it out, involved a leisurely lifestyle in a nice house in the suburbs, with two kids and one white West Highland terrier. Nagato silently watched me as I read. A keen sense of the absurdity of what I was doing rose up within me.

It *was* stupid.

I stopped my emotionless reading. If I had to read any more of this nonsense, I'd go crazy. I'd never reach any kind of understanding with Nakagawa. There could be no relationship with anyone who possessed a mind capable of putting forth such oppressive lines. No wonder we were never close friends in junior high. He'd fallen in love at first sight, let it stew for half a year, then suddenly had a messenger deliver an insane love confession—he was beyond help.

"Yeah, so, it goes on like that for a while, but you get the point, right?"

To which Nagato replied, "Understood," and nodded.

Seriously?

I looked at her, and she looked at me.

Time passed quietly, as though the very word "silence" had sprouted wings and was flying around us.

"..."

Nagato tilted her head just slightly but took no other action, simply fixing me in her gaze. So, uh, what now? Was I supposed to say something?

As I was riffling through my vocabulary for a response—

"Message received."

Her gaze never wavered.

"But I cannot comply." Her voice was as calm as always. "There is no guarantee that I will remain autonomous for the next ten years," she said, then closed her mouth. Her expression did not change. Her eyes did not move away from me.

"Yeah..."

I looked away first, pretending to shake my head just to look away from those deep, dark eyes that threatened to suck me in.

"Yeah, I guess so. Ten years is too long for anyone."

There were other problems with the confession besides the length of time, but for the time being I was relieved. As to where this sense of relief came from, the short version is that I didn't care if it was Nakagawa or not—I didn't want to see Nagato walking around with some other guy. I can't deny that the image of the way Nagato looked back when Haruhi disappeared had stuck with me. It wasn't that Nakagawa was a bad guy — he was actually okay — it's just that I couldn't forget Nagato's distressed face as she pulled softly on my sleeve.

"Sorry, Nagato."

I crumpled up the loose-leaf slip.

"This is really my fault. I shouldn't have so faithfully written down all that stuff. I should've just told Nakagawa 'no' when he called me. Just forget all about this. I'll give that moron a good talking-to. He's not really the type to turn into a stalker, so you don't have to worry about that."

Of course, if Asahina were to get a boyfriend, I'd probably wind up stalking him.

Wait — Ah, so that's how it was.

I realized what the hazy feeling in my chest was.

To put it bluntly, I didn't like the idea of some other guy getting between Asahina and me or Nagato and me. It just bothered me — hence my relief. I guess I was pretty transparent.

What about Haruhi? I didn't have to worry about her. She rejected any guy who got close to her. If there were some kind of natural disaster and Haruhi actually started going out with someone, she wouldn't be constantly looking for aliens and time travelers, would be nice to Earth, and would make things easier for Koizumi too.

And the craziness I seemed to be constantly getting tangled up in would come to an end too, surely. Perhaps that day would actually come, but it definitely wasn't here yet.

I opened the window. The sharp winter chill cut through the indoor air, which had been warmed by our body heat. I wound up and chucked the crumpled-up ball of paper as far out the window as I could.

The ball caught the wind and traced a steep arc down. It soon fell in the grassy area beside the covered path that led to the clubroom. I imagined it'd be blown along the ground, winding up in one of the gutters that ran along the school buildings, and eventually decompose along with the rotting leaves.

How wrong I was.

"Oh, shi—"

Just then, a person walking down the covered path to the club-room changed direction and made for the grassy area. She looked up and glared at me as though I'd tossed a cigarette butt, then strode over and picked up the paper I'd just tossed.

"Hey, stop! Don't look at that!"

Ignoring my protests, she picked up the trash that no one had asked her to pick up and, uncrumpling the paper, began to read.

"…"

Nagato continued to regard me wordlessly.

I know it's sudden, but let's put on our thinking caps.

Question 1: What was written on that paper?
Answer: A confession of love for Nagato.

Question 2: In whose handwriting was it written?
Answer: Mine.

Question 3: What would happen if some uninformed third party read it?
Answer: They would probably get the wrong idea.

Question 4: What if Haruhi read it?
Answer: I don't even want to think about that.

Thus did Haruhi Suzumiya scan the paper intently for a few minutes, eventually looking back up to me sharply, then for some reason grinning unpleasantly.

… That cinched it. Today was not my day.

* * *

Just ten seconds later, she had already burst into the clubroom with ferocious speed and seized me by the collar.

"What the hell are you thinking? Are you an idiot? I'm gonna set you straight this instant—jump out the window! Now!" she shouted with a grin. That grin looked pretty forced, but if you converted the force with which she dragged me to the open window, it'd be enough to power a heater all day. She didn't let up even a little as I frantically tried to think of the words I could use to explain the situation.

"No, look, this is—there's this guy I knew from junior high named Nakagawa, and he—"

"What, you're gonna try to make this someone else's fault? You wrote this, didn't you?"

Haruhi dragged me along, then stared right in my face from maybe ten centimeters away, her eyes large and clear.

"Just let me go. This is no way to have a conversation."

Just as I was wrestling with Haruhi, a fourth person appeared, his or her timing seriously bad.

"...Wha—"

Asahina's eyes were as big as saucers as she stood in the open doorway, then she covered her mouth elegantly.

"...Um...are you busy? Maybe I should, er, come back later..."

We were at each other's throats, but that didn't really count as "busy." There wasn't anything fun about wrestling with Haruhi, and if I had to wrestle, I'd take Asahina, thanks—so come on. I'd never once denied Asahina the right to enter, nor did I plan to.

Anyway, Nagato was sitting right there doing nothing, so there wasn't any reason why Asahina couldn't come in too. And I'd owe her one if she could help me out of this.

I tried to smile at Asahina as I grappled with Haruhi.

"My goodness."

The last brigade member had arrived, and he stood next to Asahina.

"Am I a bit early, perhaps?"

Koizumi smiled brightly and brushed his hair aside.

"Asahina, it seems we're intruding here. It's best not to interfere in domestic quarrels, so perhaps we should excuse ourselves for the time being and return once things are settled. I'll treat you to a coffee from the vending machine."

Hang on, Koizumi. If he thought this was some kind of lovers' quarrel, he needed to get his eyesight checked. And don't use this to abduct Asahina either — this is no time for her to be nodding in agreement with you!

Haruhi had grabbed my shirt with her madman's strength while I gripped her wrist. At this rate I was going to tear a muscle, so I called out for help.

"Hey, wait, Koizumi! Where are you going? Help me out!"

"Hmm, what to do?"

Koizumi decided this was the time to play dumb, while Asahina cowered like a scared rabbit, blinking rapidly. She didn't seem to notice Koizumi putting his arm around her waist as though escorting her somewhere.

When I looked to see what Nagato was doing, she was unsurprisingly reading her book, as though none of this had anything to do with her. This was all about her to begin with, so couldn't she spare a few words of explanation?

Haruhi's grip tightened.

"I'm such a dope, letting someone into my brigade who's so stupid that they wrote a ridiculous letter like this. I should resign in shame! I feel like I stuck my foot into a shoe filled with roaches!"

Despite her anger, Haruhi was still smiling incomprehensibly. It was as though she didn't know what expression to use in a situation like this.

"I'd already thought up thirteen different punishments before I got here! First, I'm gonna make you jump on top of a wall with a dried mackerel in your mouth and make you fight for territory with the rest of the alley cats! And you'll have to wear cat ears!"

Now if Asahina had worn cat ears with her maid outfit, that would've been something to see, but if I did it, I'd get hauled off in one of those legendary super ambulances.

"We're fresh out of cat ears."

I looked toward the open window and sighed.

Sorry, Nakagawa. If I didn't spill my guts, I'd wind up getting tossed out that window just like your love letter. It wasn't what I'd wanted to do, but if Haruhi's misunderstanding wasn't cleared up, it could mean trouble for the whole of the natural world.

I looked into the brigade chief's eyes and used the same calm tone I used when trying to calm Shamisen as I trimmed his claws.

"Listen. First, put me down. Haruhi—let me explain things. I'll make it clear enough to get through even your thick skull, all right?"

Ten minutes later.

"Hmph."

Haruhi sat cross-legged on a folding chair, sipping a cup of hot green tea.

"You've got some weird friends. I mean, he can fall in love at first sight all he wants, but the letter's going too far. It's so stupid."

Love could cause brain damage as well as make someone blind. Not that I disagreed with her last statement, though.

Haruhi held up the wrinkled piece of notebook paper and waved it around.

"I thought for sure you'd teamed up with that moron Taniguchi to give Yuki a hard time. It's the kind of thing he'd do, and Yuki's so quiet. She'd be easy to fool."

I figured there wasn't anyone less easy to fool than Nagato

anywhere in the galaxy, but I listened without interrupting. Haruhi seemed to notice me exercising my self-control and gave me a glare before her features relaxed.

"No, I guess you wouldn't do that. You don't have the cunning for this kind of thing."

I wasn't sure if she was complimenting me or just being nasty, but at least she didn't think I would do the kind of thing a thoughtless elementary school kid would pull. And even Taniguchi had a reasonable amount of discretion for his age.

"Still…"

It was the angelic pride of the SOS Brigade that lit the fuse.

"…It's lovely, isn't it?"

Asahina spoke in a dreamy voice.

"If someone were like that over me, I think I'd be kind of happy. Ten years? I'd love to meet someone who would wait ten years for me. It's so romantic…"

She clasped her hands, her eyes shining.

I wasn't completely sure if Asahina's definition of "romantic" was the same as the one I'd learned or not, but it didn't seem to be. Maybe some words' definitions have changed in the future. And she was the kind of person who didn't understand how boats floated until you explained it to her.

Incidentally, Asahina was just wearing her school uniform today. We'd taken the maid outfit, nurse outfit, and all the other costumes to the cleaners—even the frog costume. When Haruhi and I had gone to the cleaners with the stack of clothes all scented with Asahina's fragrance, the old man behind the counter had given us both a stare so unnecessarily hard that I felt a little traumatized afterward.

"True romance and Nakagawa are worlds apart."

I swallowed the last of the tea in my teacup and continued.

"Trust me, he's a big, thick guy who'd never in a million years wind up as the hero of a girls' romance comic. In animal

fortune-telling terms, he'd be a bear with a crescent moon on his chest."

As I spoke, I thought of ad copy to perfectly match the image I had of him from junior high.

"Yeah, like a gentle giant," I said.

I didn't have much to go on, but that was the image that came to mind. His physique was well-developed, anyway. In a different sense than Asahina's, I mean.

I should've apologized to Nakagawa for this, but soon Haruhi had given a dramatic reading of the words he'd dictated to me—I didn't have the stamina for such a reading—and Koizumi's impression was rather different from Asahina's.

"That was an excellent composition, I must say."

His smile was as pretentious as ever.

"Above all, it was concrete. While it was a bit too idealistic, the honest way in which he's clearly looking at reality is appealing. One does get the sense that he's lost himself in the passion of the moment, but reading between the lines, one can feel his rising spirit and heart. If he keeps up the effort, this Mr. Nakagawa will become a formidable man indeed."

It sounded like something a cut-rate psychoanalyst would say. There was a limit to what you could say about other people's lives, I thought. I could think of all kinds of things to say, as long as I didn't actually have to take any responsibility for them. What was he, a bogus fortune-teller?

"However—"

Koizumi smiled again.

"He certainly is bold, composing a letter like this. And you're a good person, too, for writing it down. I'm afraid my fingers would've refused to do it."

Was that a roundabout way of giving me a hard time? Well, unlike you, I actually care about my friends. At least enough to play part-time Cupid, even when I knew what the outcome would be.

I shrugged and gave Koizumi my reply.

"Nagato told me her response before you guys got here."

I spoke for Nagato, who was paying equal amounts of attention to Haruhi and Koizumi.

"Ten years is too long, she says. I mean, of course it is, right? That's what I'd say too."

Then, after having been silent the entire time, Nagato spoke.

"Let me see."

She reached out with slender fingers.

Now that was unusual, I thought. Haruhi seemed to think so too.

"Oh yeah? So you're interested, are you?" she said, peering past the unevenly cut bangs of the sole member of the literature club. "Kyon's the one who wrote it down, but you should hang on to it anyway, as a memento. You don't see this kind of half-direct, half-roundabout love confession much nowadays."

"Here you go."

Koizumi took the wrinkled paper from Haruhi and passed it to Nagato.

"…"

Nagato lowered her eyes and read the words I had written, over and over, her eyes flicking up and down over the same lines, as if silently digesting their contents.

"I cannot wait."

Well, of course.

But Nagato continued.

"I will see him."

The room fell silent at her statement, and then, as if to deliver a final blow to my slackened jaw:

"I am interested," she said, looking at me. Her eyes looked the way they always did.

I knew those eyes well—honest, pure, like handcrafted glass pieces.

*　　*　　*

The big cleaning day wound up being a normal cleaning day. When I suggested we dispose of the books on the bookshelves, Nagato didn't give me a straight "yes" or "no," but just stared at me with a vague sadness that left me unable to say anything more, and the only game from Koizumi's collection we threw away was a cheap dice game from a magazine that we'd played only once anyway.

Asahina didn't have any personal items save her tea set. And the disposal of anything that Haruhi had brought in was met with a flat "No!"

"Now listen here, Kyon. I don't ever waste anything I can use. If it can be reused, it should be, and so long as it's holding together, I won't throw it away. That's the spirit of environmentalism!"

I wondered if this was how hoarders got started on their hoarding. If you wanted to be an environmentalist, you shouldn't do anything but the minimum for survival, I thought.

Haruhi tied a kerchief over her hair and had Nagato and Asahina do likewise, giving them a mop and a duster, while Koizumi and I got buckets and washcloths along with orders to wash the windows.

"This will be the last time we're here this year, so in order to face the new year with a nice, clean feeling, we're going home with the place sparkling."

Thus ordered, Koizumi and I got to work on the windows. After a while, I glanced at the trio of girls, wondering whether they were cleaning the room or just spreading dust around, when my cleaning partner spoke quietly.

"This is just between you and me, but there are other organizations besides the Agency trying to get close to Nagato. Right now she's every bit as important as you and Suzumiya. Nagato is in a unique position even among her fellow humanoid interfaces, which is probably a recent development."

I sat on the windowsill and breathed on my wet hand to warm

it up while washing with the other hand; the winter chill robbed them of warmth all too quickly.

What the hell was this—

It was easy to play dumb. Recently I'd had experiences with both Nagato and Asahina that had nothing to do with Haruhi or Koizumi, and as a result I was still here, so I couldn't just ignore this.

"I'll figure something out," I answered casually.

This whole situation had been caused by me. I'd have to be the one to fix it.

"Indeed. I'm counting on you. I have my hands quite full with planning the SOS Brigade's winter mountain trip. And may I just say that while you can release stress by quarreling with Suzumiya, I have no such sparring partner."

Who was the tomcat now?

But the handsome smile on Koizumi's face twisted.

"Isn't it about time for me to take off this harmless-looking mask and change the character I've been playing for so long? It's quite tiring being so polite to my classmates all the time."

If it was so tiring, he should've just stopped. I have no desire to control how he talked, I told him.

"That won't do at all. My current self fits with the image Suzumiya wishes. I'm quite a specialist in her psychology."

Koizumi gave an exaggerated sigh.

"On that count, I am rather envious of Asahina. After all, she needn't change a single thing about herself."

Didn't he once say that Asahina's manner might be an act? I asked him.

"Oh, did you really believe what I said? If I've actually won your trust, perhaps there's been some value in all this effort."

As evasive as ever. His untrustworthy speech patterns hadn't changed all year. Even Nagato had undergone some internal changes, but Koizumi was the same as always. For Asahina's part, she didn't need to change. I'd met the other Asahina, so I knew for certain that she'd mature both physically and psychologically.

"If I were to change somehow…"

Koizumi wiped more vigorously.

"…that would not be a good sign. The status quo is my duty. I can't imagine you'd want to see me look serious."

You're right, I wouldn't, I told him. His grinning face was perfectly suited to cleaning up Haruhi's messes or setting things up for her in advance. I was really looking forward to whatever play waited for us in the snowy mountains. That is enough, right? I said.

"I can't imagine a finer compliment. I'll accept that."

I didn't know whether he meant it or not, but in any case his words ended up as white condensation on the window.

Later that evening.

Shamisen was curled up on my bed, and I looked at his sleeping face, feeling warm and pleasant. I wondered where this pleasant feeling came from and pondered the particular distinctions between love and lust. Just as I felt I was upon an answer —

"Kyon, telephone! The boy from yesterday!"

Once again my sister opened the door to my room, holding the receiver.

She handed me the receiver, which was playing some easy listening version of a famous classical tune, then she sat on the edge of the bed and began tugging at Shamisen's whiskers.

"Shami, Shami, Shami's so furry, Mommy's gonna…"

I watched Shamisen open his eyes slightly to glare at, then ignore, my sister, then watched my happily singing sister as I put the phone to my ear. What had I been thinking about earlier? I wondered.

"Hello?"

"It's me."

My junior high classmate Nakagawa couldn't hide the urgency he was feeling.

"How did it go? What was her answer? You gotta tell me. I don't care what it was; I'm ready to hear it. C'mon, Kyon, out with it...!"

He sounded like a politician up for reelection, desperately listening to the news of the results.

"Unfortunately, I couldn't get a favorable answer."

I looked to my sister and shushed her as I tried to sound grim.

"She said she won't wait. She said that she can't imagine what will happen in ten years, that there are no guarantees."

Since I was just relaying the facts, the words came smoothly. But just as I was wondering what to do about Nagato's problematic statement that she would see him—

"I see."

Nakagawa's voice was surprisingly calm.

"I guess I'm not surprised. I didn't think she would agree that easily either."

I kept waving my head, and my strangely singing sister groaned her irritation before hauling Shamisen off the bed and leaving the room. She was probably going to go sleep with him in her own room, but give it an hour and Shamisen would probably come slinking back to my room. Cats didn't like being given too much attention.

Once my sister left, I put my question to the phone.

"That's all you have to say after making me read out that humiliating letter?"

If he had anticipated that reply, he shouldn't have asked me to deliver the message.

"I realize that getting a heartfelt declaration of love from a complete stranger is bound to be difficult," he said.

If you realized that, then don't do it! You had to have a pretty obscure hobby indeed to go around knowingly stepping on land mines.

"But this should have at least piqued her interest a bit."

You have to be at least a little impressed at Nakagawa's plan. It was true that he was the first one to get Nagato to say she was interested. His message had had enough power to do that much, anyway. It's enough to make me want to guarantee that he's currently the most shameless guy on the planet.

"So about that, Kyon. I have another favor to ask."

What was it now? My spirit of community service was at low ebb.

"Did you know I joined the football team when I started high school? I mean American football, not soccer."

"That is the first I've heard of it," I said.

"Ah. Well, I did. And that's the favor I need. My team is going to host another school's team for a game. I want you to bring Nagato to watch. I'm a first-stringer, of course."

"When?"

"Tomorrow."

I really didn't need another person like Haruhi in my life. Why were their schedules always so cramped?

"If Nagato won't wait ten years for me, there's nothing I can do about that. If it's come to this, I'll have to show off some heroics and get her attention that way."

Such a simplistic notion. He could've given a little thought to my position, at least—or at least thought about how busy the end of the year was.

"Is it not convenient for you?"

It wasn't inconvenient. I had no plans tomorrow at all. Nagato probably didn't either. It wasn't inconvenient at all, so at this rate I was probably going to get sucked into watching his "heroics" or whatever. I told him as much.

"Great. Please come. It's a friendly game, but we're going to play for keeps. Our football team plays the school from the next town over every year. The outcome of the game is going to determine whether or not we have a pleasant new year. If we lose, it's going to be the winter vacation from hell. There won't be a break for New Year's Eve or New Year's Day. It'll just be more practice."

Nakagawa sounded serious, even pathetic, but it wasn't my problem. I told him that there was a pile of annoying things I needed to take care of by the end of the year. There weren't many days before the mountain trip, after all.

"Kyon, I don't care about whatever plans you have. What's important is Nagato. Please, just ask her. If she refuses, then I'll give up. But so long as there's even one chance in a thousand, I'll take that chance. Dreams will always stay mere dreams without action."

That sounded like a load of nonsense to me, but I couldn't bring myself to say it — my old weakness.

"Fine," I said.

I flopped down on the bed and sighed.

"I'll call Nagato after this."

I had a premonition. Nagato would not refuse.

"Where was your school again? If Nagato says okay, I'll bring her over."

I'd probably bring some other people too — that was all right, wasn't it?

"You're a great matchmaker! I'll be calling on you again for the wedding — no, perhaps I'll name our first child for you —"

"Bye," I said coldly, then hung up. If I let Nakagawa go on, I felt like worms would start coming out of my brain.

I put the cordless phone receiver on the shelf and got out my cell phone, then looked up Nagato's number and gave her a call.

The next day came very quickly.

"You're late! You're the one who called us out here, and you're the last to arrive? Do you even care about this?"

Haruhi smiled and pointed at me. We were at the station where the SOS Brigade always met. Three others were also waiting for me—Nagato, Koizumi, and Asahina.

My original idea had been to just bring the silent android along with me, but going to the game with just the two of us simply wasn't possible. I didn't even want to think about what punishment awaited us if the brigade chief found out we'd done something without her. Everyone would have to come along. After I'd called Nagato to get her answer, I called up the other three to invite them along as well. The fact that everybody had come said a lot about how much free time we all had, thanks to winter vacation. Or maybe they just wanted to see what kind of guy would fall in love with Nagato at first sight.

Owing to the midwinter chill, everyone had bundled up. Asahina's outfit was particularly notable—the fluffy furriness of her white synthetic fur coat made her look as lovely as an innocent white bunny rabbit hopping through the mountain snow. She was the one people should be falling in love with.

Nagato wore a simple duffle coat over her school uniform, the hood drawn over her head. Unsurprisingly, the pseudo-alien was able to handle our Earth's chill.

"…"

Her face was so expressionless you'd never have guessed she was going to see the guy who'd confessed his love for her.

"All right, let's go! I can't wait to see what this guy looks like. Also, it'll be my first time watching a football game!"

Haruhi wasn't the only one who seemed like she was up for a picnic. Asahina and Koizumi were both smiling. My own face was hollow, and Nagato's was blank.

"I checked the bus map in advance. It's about thirty minutes to the boys' school from here. Here's the entrance."

With a voice like a tour guide, Koizumi showed us the way. I had less and less to say.

They sure seemed to be having fun—Koizumi and Haruhi, and maybe Asahina too.

As we walked, Koizumi casually drew alongside me and whispered significantly into my ear.

"You certainly do have some mysterious friends."

I waited for him to say more, but he only smiled and went back to his role as tour guide.

Nakagawa was mysterious? Maybe. One thing was certain—no ordinary person would take one look at Nagato and be instantly struck down with love.

As we made our way to the bus station, something felt amiss about it all.

I had a bad feeling about this.

After half an hour of bouncing along on a private bus, it was a few minutes' walk from the bus stop to Nakagawa's school. When we got there, the game had already started.

Thanks to my oversleeping, we'd missed two earlier buses, and it was now fifteen minutes past the start time Nakagawa had given me.

It didn't seem like we could enter the school grounds, so we walked alongside it until coming to a field enclosed by a chain-link fence, which was where the football scrimmage was being held.

"Wow, it's such a big field."

Asahina gave voice to her wonder, and I had to nod. Unlike North High's grounds, dug forcibly out of the hillside, the flat, expansive field of this private boys' school spoke of money. The place where we were standing was roughly one floor higher than the level of the field, which gave us an excellent view. Aside from us five, there seemed to be a few old guys passing by and some girls who seemed to be groupies, cheering on the two private schools' teams.

The sound of colliding uniforms and helmets in blue and white reached our ears, and we five lined up in an empty spot to watch.

Nagato was silent and betrayed no reaction.

Even now.

I had only a casual understanding of the rules of football. After our mostly effortless victory in the baseball tournament, Haruhi had brought in forms for participation in the football and soccer tournaments. We wound up not participating in either (after much hassle), but just in case, I'd gone and looked up the basics. It seemed simple but was actually quite deep—not impossibly so, but hardly something a club like ours could just pick up and do, I could tell.

Watching from here, I could tell that my decision had been a correct one.

The offense carried an oblong ball similar to a rugby ball and tried to advance down the field by passing and running with it, while the defense tried to stop that advance by chasing down the guy with the ball, their protective gear clattering loudly whenever they collided with one another.

It definitely felt like an American sport.

"Huh."

Haruhi clung to the chain-link fence and watched the clump of players.

"So which one is Nakagawa?"

"Number eighty-two on the white team."

I explained according to what Nakagawa had told me the previous day. Nakagawa was a tight end, which meant he was at the edge of the offensive line, responsible for both blocking and catching passes. Nakagawa was quick despite his bulk, so it was the perfect spot for him.

"Wait—why are the players trading places? They look the same."

"There are offensive players and defensive players. Nakagawa's on offense."

"Since everybody's wearing helmets, I'm sure they're allowed to head-butt, but how far does it go? Only judo throws? Or does anything go?"

"None of that. No head-butting either," I said.

"Huh."

Haruhi gazed at the field intently. North High didn't have a football team, but if it did, there was no question she'd try to get on and wreak havoc. And with her speed and blind energy, she might even have been a worthwhile player.

"It sure is an exciting sport! Perfect for winter."

I listened to Haruhi's commentary and took a look at Nagato, who was following the ball, evidently not thinking about anything in particular.

The five of us stood there and watched private school boys smash into one another for a while.

"Um, would anyone like some tea?"

Asahina took a thermos and some paper cups out of her bag.

"I thought it would be cold, so I brought something warm to drink."

The smiling Asahina might as well have been an angel. I thankfully accepted her tea. I had only been getting colder as we stood out there beneath the chilly sky, watching the game.

There we watched the two teams play football, sipping Asahina's delicious hand-brewed tea.

The second quarter came to a desultory end as we sat there and watched; it was now halftime. The white uniforms of Nakagawa and his teammates coalesced at the opposite end of the field from us, where a tough-looking older guy started chewing them out. It was hard to make out faces from that distance, but I did catch occasional glimpses of jersey number eighty-two.

As for the game, it wasn't anything special. There were no long, showy passes or thirty-yard runs; each team just kept creeping along with first downs, and the score represented only the handful of field goals they'd managed; there hadn't been any touchdowns. That might have meant they were evenly matched and that the defenses were both working hard.

However, I do know a certain someone who hates it when things get boring, and her name is Haruhi Suzumiya.

"This isn't much fun at all," she said.

Haruhi stomped her feet as she frowned. She wasn't the only one whose breath was coming out white either.

"At least the players get to run around." Haruhi wrapped her arms around herself. "But we're just standing here getting cold. Is there a café around here somewhere?"

The picnic mood seemed to have been blown away by the chilly winter wind. Asahina did not have an infinite amount of tea, and we'd long since run out. And even when we'd had it, the last half had gone cold before we could finish it, irrespective of the amount of love she'd made it with, so it wasn't much good for warming up. Even worse, today marked the arrival of the coldest cold front of the winter, and Haruhi wasn't the only one whose teeth were chattering from the chill; Koizumi, Asahina, and I were right there with her. The only one who didn't seem to mind was Nagato, who never seemed to care what the temperature was.

"I guess it's really no fun unless you're playing. Maybe I should get them to let me join the game. I bet I could throw that ball."

Haruhi squinted her eyes in the face of the wind that tried to rob her of body heat.

"And if I don't do something like that, I'm just gonna freeze here. Kyon, do you have anything? Like hand warmers?"

If I had, I would've been using them myself. If she wanted to warm herself up that badly, she could've run laps around the school grounds or played Red Rover. That made the most economic and environmental sense.

"Hmph. Fine then, I've got a perfectly nice hand warmer right here. Human-size too!"

Haruhi slowly came up behind Asahina and embraced her, wrapping her arms around the poor girl's delicate neck.

"Wha—what're you—?"

Asahina was unsurprisingly dismayed.

"Ooh, Mikuru, you're so warm! And soft too!"

Haruhi buried her chin in the unsullied snowlike fur of Asahina's collar, embracing the petite (and occasionally abundant) figure of her upperclassman.

"I think I'll stay like this awhile. Hee hee, are you jealous, Kyon?"

You're damn right I was. Although if I had my choice, I would've wanted to hug her from the front.

"Hmm?"

Haruhi pursed her lips.

"Wh—"

She cut herself off, then took a breath.

"So, with Mikuru, then?"

I looked back and forth between Haruhi's mischievous face and Asahina's terrified eyes as the former held her embrace on the latter, and I tried to think of a way to answer. From behind me, my rescue appeared.

"Would you like to play Red Rover with me, then?"

Butting into the conversation, the disgusting Koizumi smiled disgustingly.

"I wouldn't mind going for a jog, but I'd also be just fine wrestling around with another man."

Well, I wasn't fine. I've said it before, but I don't bat for that team. Koizumi should've stuck to giving football commentary. This was all about me, Nagato, and Nakagawa, anyway—Koizumi was just a bonus. In fact, given the circumstances, Asahina and Haruhi were bonuses too.

I gave him a sidelong glare.

"I couldn't care less."

The central character for the day—Nagato—was as silent as always, unmoving as she watched the field. I got the feeling she was following Nakagawa with her eyes, but there was no way to know for sure.

Meanwhile, Nakagawa never once looked our way, whether he was moving around the field as part of the offensive line or sitting on the sidelines. I'd gone to all the trouble of bringing Nagato out here and now—nothing? Even now, during halftime, he was gathered with his teammates in a circle as they had a serious-seeming meeting. Had his desire for victory won out over all other considerations?

Or was this all on purpose? If the things he'd said were true, he'd been struck completely dumb upon seeing Nagato from a distance. I'd thought that had to be an exaggeration, but if it were true, he definitely wouldn't want to be stricken thusly during the game.

"Eh, whatever," I muttered, looking at the back of Nagato's head as the wind brushed the nape of her neck.

I guessed we could meet up with Nakagawa once the game was over and he came out of the school. If the second half ended smoothly, Nakagawa's team would win and he'd be free.

The previous day, Nagato had said she wouldn't mind seeing him, so having them meet up wouldn't bother anybody. Truth be told, I wasn't thrilled with the idea, but that didn't mean I was so callous as to mercilessly crush somebody else's hopes and dreams. I could hear a guy out, after all.

And yet.

Unfortunately, things did not go smoothly. The whistle signaling the resumption of play had blown, and we were about five minutes into the third quarter when—

Nakagawa was taken away in an ambulance.

*　　*　　*

Allow me to describe the circumstances of his injury. It went something like this.

The second half began with the opposing team's kickoff. The returner got tackled at his own twenty-yard line, whereupon it was time for Nakagawa's team to take the offense.

The teams lined up and hunched down at the line of scrimmage; Nakagawa was at the far edge. In the center, the white-uniformed quarterback seemed to call out some kind of signal to his left and right. At the signal, Nakagawa moved sideways along the line. At the same time, the quarterback received the ball and took two or three steps back as the tackles and linebackers of the defense came rushing forward like wild beasts.

Nakagawa sprinted, heading to the inside—he then turned and moved as though he were receiving a pass. But it was a fake—the quarterback flicked his wrist and sent the ball past Nakagawa to the wide receiver.

"Oh—!"

I wasn't sure whether Haruhi or Asahina had raised her voice in surprise.

The ball spun like a bullet shot from a rifle, but the trajectory was a bit off. An opposing linebacker made a desperate jump but couldn't quite manage the interception. Nakagawa's team narrowly avoided a turnover as the ball brushed his fingers, but that was enough to perturb its path.

Just then—

I saw Nagato, up until that point as still as a bodhisattva's statue, move her hand.

"..."

She drew her hood over her head, tugging it down a bit to obscure her line of sight. But from what of her face I could still see, I could tell that her lips were moving.

"—"

She was definitely muttering something—and fast too.

I only caught it out of the corner of my eye, since my attention was on the field.

"Whoa—"

I leaned forward, eyes widening.

I thought the ball had only been deflected slightly, but then I realized that its destination was the place where Nakagawa was currently dashing to at top speed. I saw him make a perfect leap, grab the ball in midair, and try to make a stable landing—

—but no.

Just as Nakagawa jumped, the cornerback who had been covering him also jumped. His goal was the same ball that every player prized nearly as much as his own life.

The cornerback had taken his broad jump just as Nakagawa was reaching the ball. As humans do not possess the wings they would need to change direction in midair, the player's energy dropped to zero as he collided with the falling Nakagawa. Given that both players bounced off of and away from each other, you can imagine how intense the impact was.

The opposing cornerback spun ninety degrees and fell onto his back, while the defenseless Nakagawa rotated a full half turn, landing perfectly vertical on his head.

"Eek!"

Asahina cried out in concern.

I yelled too. Nakagawa had clearly landed in the worst possible way for a human being to land—like a pro wrestler who receives a Tombstone Piledriver or Sukekiyo in *The Inugami Clan*. But at least wrestlers had the mat, and Sukekiyo had the swamp. All Nakagawa had under him was the hard, cold earth.

Lagging just behind the sight came the sound—a sound nobody ever wants to hear.

Thok!

If he was lucky, that dull crack was the sound of his helmet splitting—otherwise it was his skull.

The referee blew his whistle and stopped the game. Nakagawa lay still. He'd stopped moving, clinging to the ball as though it were some precious memento from his parents—no, he hadn't moved at all. This wasn't even funny anymore.

"Is he going to be okay?"

Haruhi clung to the fence, her brow furrowed.

"Eek—"

Asahina half hid herself behind Haruhi's shoulder, as though turning away from a violent scene in a horror movie.

"Oh...there's the stretcher..." she said, her voice tremulous.

Surrounded by his teammates, Nakagawa's prone form was quickly moved to the stretcher and taken to the sidelines. His determination admirable, he still clung to the ball. The scene was so moving, it would be unbelievable if his team didn't now rally and defeat their opponents.

Lying there on the stretcher with his helmet removed, Nakagawa seemed to have dodged the bullet. He opened his eyes in response to the calls of the people around him, nodding to answer their questions. He tried to sit up, only collapsed back down, but at the very least he was still breathing.

"Probably a minor concussion."

Koizumi made his diagnosis.

"I doubt there's much to worry about. These things happen in sports like this."

I didn't know where he got off making that call from a distance, and not being a doctor to begin with. Hopefully he was right, but the head is a bad place to take an impact. The coach and faculty advisor seemed just as concerned as I was, and soon the wailing siren of an ambulance approached.

"Your friend has rotten luck," said Haruhi, sounding regretful. "He tries to show off to Yuki and gets injured instead. Maybe he got too eager."

She sounded sympathetic. Did she really want Nakagawa and

Nagato to hit it off? Even though she'd slammed the door in the computer club president's face when he'd wanted to borrow Nagato?

I asked her as much, to which she replied, "Listen, Kyon. I think that love is a kind of disease, but I'm not going to interfere in other people's love lives just for kicks. Everybody has their own path to happiness."

I shrugged, letting Haruhi's overlong philosophy of romance go in one ear and out the other. Sorry—if Asahina's boyfriend turned out to be a loser, I don't care how happy she seemed, I wasn't confident I'd be able to be happy for her. I might even try to interfere. I don't think anybody could blame me, though.

"I hope your friend is all right."

Asahina clasped her hands together in front of her fluffy fur coat, an expression of true concern on her face. She definitely wasn't faking it. That's just the kind of person she was. Her prayers could heal you in half an hour even if every bone in your body was broken. I was sure Nakagawa would be fine.

The ambulance finally arrived, and Nakagawa was loaded into it, as carefully as though he were a cardboard box marked FRAGILE—HANDLE WITH CARE.

As soon as he was inside the ambulance and the doors were shut behind him, the siren blared back to life, the almost painfully bright flashing lights winking red as it headed off into the distance.

"..."

Nagato had been at least 50 percent less voluble than even she normally was, and she watched the ambulance go, as though trying to confirm the existence of redshift with her own dark eyes.

So, what next?

Nakagawa's demonstration was unavoidably canceled thanks to his withdrawal, but with his departure went our desire to watch the rest of the scrimmage. It was freezing cold, after all, and our primary reason for standing here would soon be arriving at the hospital.

"Shouldn't we go to the hospital too?"

Haruhi spoke suddenly.

"He was our whole reason for coming, and that's where he's going, so if we follow him, we can see how this turns out. It'll be a great scene, with the worried Yuki going to visit him at his bedside! I'll bet he'd be really moved. Plus, the hospital will be heated. Whaddaya think?"

She obviously thought it was a grand idea, but I didn't really feel like entering a hospital for a while. I've been sustaining trauma ever since meeting Haruhi.

"Aren't you worried about your friend? Let me tell you, when you got taken away in an ambulance, I definitely worried about you. You know, a certain amount."

Haruhi dragged me along by the arm, her tone brusque.

"Honestly, you caused so much trouble."

She walked a few steps with me, then stopped.

"By the way, which hospital did that ambulance go to?"

How the hell was I supposed to know?

"I'll look into it," said Koizumi, brandishing his cell phone with a smile. "This will just take a moment."

Koizumi turned his back to us and walked a few steps away, then pushed a button on his phone and had a quiet exchange with whomever he'd called. Maybe a minute later, he flipped his phone closed, then turned back to us and smiled.

"I've found his destination."

I didn't know who he'd called, but I'd bet it wasn't 911.

"It's a hospital we know quite well. I doubt I need to tell you how to get there."

A wave of memory hit me, my mind recalling the white of the sheets and the red of the apples. Koizumi smiled at me.

"Yes, that's the one. The general hospital you were taken to not so long ago."

As in, the one where his uncle's friend was the director. I glared at Koizumi. This had better be a coincidence.

"It's a coincidence."

Koizumi chuckled as he saw my thousand-yard stare.

"No, it really is. Quite unexpected. Honestly, I'm quite surprised myself."

I didn't trust him anyway, so his trustworthy smile was wasted on me.

"All right, let's go to the hospital. Can we get a cab somewhere? With five of us, we can split the fare and it'll be cheap." Haruhi immediately started lining things up.

"Suzumiya, I was thinking that we should have a meeting regarding the upcoming trip to the mountains. We'll leave the hospital visit to these two, while you, Asahina, and I nail down the details of the trip. We haven't sorted out things like luggage, precise dates, and so on, and we need to finalize these details."

Haruhi wobbled midstep at Koizumi's statement. "Oh, really?"

"Yes," said Koizumi, continuing. "New Year's Eve is right around the corner. A holiday in a snowy mountain lodge is a big event. Honestly, I'd planned to hold the SOS Brigade's winter trip meeting today, but some unexpected things came up."

Well, excuse me, I said.

"Not at all. But in exchange, I'll leave Nagato in your hands. You should hurry to the hospital and check in on Mr. Nakagawa. Regarding what to do there, I'll leave that to your discretion. Asahina, Suzumiya, and I will be in our usual café. Will that do, Suzumiya?"

Haruhi pursed her lips and frowned.

"Mmm, I guess so. There's definitely no point in me going to the hospital. Kyon's friend only cares about Yuki."

She looked a little irritated, though.

"All right, Kyon. You go with Yuki to see your friend. If he can write a love letter like that, he'll probably jump right out of the hospital bed after he sees Yuki for five seconds."

But then she pointed at me harshly.

"But! You'd better tell me everything that happens! Got that?" she said with a half-angry, half-amused expression.

We took a bus back to our rendezvous point, then split into two groups to go our separate ways—Nagato and I would change buses to head to the hospital, while Haruhi and the rest would continue to be regulars at the nearby café.

Nagato never looked back, so I was determined to. I saw Haruhi and the others watching us go, with Haruhi making some kind of strange gestures as she walked. Not wanting to imagine what her body language was suggesting, I soon looked to my companion, bundled up in her duffle coat.

So, then.

I'll put it simply. Worries encrusted my mind like barnacles. I was worried enough about Nakagawa, who'd gotten injured just as he was trying to impress Nagato, but I was even more concerned about what Koizumi had said: "You certainly do have some mysterious friends." The "mysterious" part especially bothered me. I didn't have any friends who were particularly exceptional, and if I had to pick one, it would be Koizumi himself. What was it about Nakagawa that he thought was so "mysterious"?

And then there was the strange incantation that Nagato had been chanting. Nakagawa's accident had happened immediately afterward, and even the dumbest person imaginable would be able to put the two events together, given the pattern so far. Yes, Nagato was quite an artist, if she could turn me into an ace reliever capable of striking out three consecutive batters.

"..."

Her face buried within the hood of her coat, Nagato said nothing—but the answer would soon be revealed.

Upon asking at the reception desk, we learned that Nakagawa had already been examined and treated, and he was now resting in a hospital room. Though not serious, his injuries apparently required observation. I headed to the room number we were given, Nagato trailing behind me like a ghost.

Hardly a "hospital room." We found Nakagawa in a six-person ward.

"Nakagawa, you doing okay?"

"Hey, Kyon."

My former classmate wore a blue hospital gown and lay there on the bed. He didn't look especially injured with his close-cropped jock haircut. He sat up like a panda awoken from a nap.

"You've got great timing. They just finished examining me. I'm gonna stay the night for observation. I kinda tweaked my neck and got a concussion when I fell, which is why I felt like I wanted to throw up. I called my coach and told him I'd be out tomorrow, so he didn't have to come visit—"

As he was talking, he noticed the ghost standing behind me. His eyes widened.

"Is that...could it be...?"

It was indeed.

"This is Nagato. Yuki Nagato. I brought her along to cheer you up."

"Aaahh—!"

Nakagawa suddenly straightened his sturdy frame, sitting bolt upright. Well, aren't you feeling healthy? I thought. Apparently his head was well enough.

"I'm Nakagawa!" he shouted by way of self-introduction. "'Naka' as in 'Chuya Nakahara,' and 'kawa' as in the Yellow

River! Humbly at your service!" He sounded like a rural daimyo at his first audience with the shogun.

"Yuki Nagato." She gave her name, her voice unmoved. She hadn't bothered to take off her duffle coat or even to pull back the hood. Unable to watch any longer, I flipped back the hood. We'd come all the way out here to meet him — it would've been a waste if he never got a proper look at her face.

The silent Nagato just stared at Nakagawa. After about ten seconds, he finally cracked.

"Huh? Um…"

Nakagawa's expression turned somehow dubious.

"You're Nagato…right?"

"Yes," said Nagato.

"The one who was walking with Kyon this spring…"

"Yes."

"At the supermarket near the station?"

"Yes."

"I…I see…"

Nakagawa's face darkened. I had expected him to cry tears of joy or faint dead away, so what was this sudden unpleasantness?

Nagato looked at Nakagawa as though he were a motionless flatfish in an aquarium, while Nakagawa regarded her as he would a manhole cover in the middle of the street.

Such a staring match can only go on so long, and sure enough, the first to turn away was Nakagawa.

"…Kyon."

He tried to speak quietly, but all the other patients in the ward would have easily heard. But he was gesturing with his finger to quietly call me closer, and I couldn't very well ignore him.

"What?"

"Listen, uh…we need to talk. About…y'know…"

I could see him constantly glancing over at Nagato. Evidently he wanted to ask something about her.

I looked over at Nagato to confirm.

"Yeah," he said.

Despite the lack of telepathy, Nagato turned around and walked out of the room as though carried by a conveyor belt.

Once he saw Nagato slide the door shut behind her, Nakagawa sighed in relief.

"Is she...really Nagato? The real one?"

I'd never seen a fake Nagato, that was for sure. I'd seen her act rather differently sometimes, but that was ancient history.

"Hey, be happier," I said. "Your future bride came to visit you—can't you show a little gratitude?"

"Uh...yeah..."

Nakagawa muttered and nodded.

"That...that was Nagato. Not a twin sister or a look-alike."

What was he trying to say? Don't tell me you need her to wear glasses, I told him. Hadn't he bumped into her recently? She quit wearing them at my request, so if he had a glasses fetish, I didn't want to hear about it.

"No, that's not it."

Nakagawa looked up at me with a pained expression.

"I can't explain it...just give me a second to think, Kyon. I'm really sorry..."

He just sat there on his hospital bed, groaning. Had that blow to the head really messed something up, after all? His reactions were incomprehensible. No matter what I said to him, he just groaned and looked up at the ceiling, as though deep in thought. Eventually he even clutched his head as though in pain. I gave up and decided to leave.

"Nakagawa, I'm gonna want to hear a reason for this eventually. What am I going to tell her?"

My report to Haruhi was going to be pointless too. If I told her the truth now, a flinty-eyed glare would be all that greeted me.

I left the hospital room, where Nagato was leaning against the hallway's wall, waiting for me. She turned her dark eyes to me for a moment, then looked back at the floor.

"Let's go."

Nagato gave a slight nod, then fell in step behind me.

Just what the hell was that all about?

I stalked tiger-beetle-like ahead of the quiet Nagato, heading for the bus terminal.

The scene that followed at the café barely merits explanation. Haruhi talked merrily away about her plans for the winter vacation, while Koizumi mechanically agreed with her. Asahina seemed to be enjoying her Darjeeling tea as she sipped it, while I sat there, discouraged, and Nagato played the role of silent listener as she watched the proceedings.

We split the bill, and today's SOS Brigade activities came to an end. When I went home, I was greeted by this:

"Oh, Kyon! Perfect timing—there's a phone call for you!"

My sister smiled, holding out the receiver with one hand while dragging Shamisen around with the other. I took both the phone and the cat and went into my room.

As I'd expected, the call was from Nakagawa.

"This is really hard to say, but…"

Nakagawa had informed me that he was calling from a pay phone at the hospital, and from the tone of his voice, he indeed sounded reluctant to continue.

"Could you give her the message that I'm withdrawing my marriage proposal?"

He sounded like a midsize company president begging for an extension on a loan.

"Want to tell me why?"

Meanwhile, I sounded like an irritated creditor facing a helpless business owner.

"After creating this one-sided fantasy, you're backing out after one day? What have you been doing the past few months? You meet Nagato face-to-face, and suddenly you're not interested? Depending on your explanation, I may not have much to say to you."

"I'm sorry. I don't really understand it myself, but..."

Nakagawa sounded genuinely contrite.

"When she rushed over to the hospital to see me, I was so happy. I should thank you for that. But when I saw her, she didn't have that luminous aura. No matter how I looked at her, she looked like an ordinary girl — no, she was an ordinary girl. I just don't understand what happened."

I thought of Nagato's face, with its uncertainty-inspiring expression.

"Kyon, I've been thinking about it, and I've finally come to a conclusion. I thought I had fallen in love with Nagato, but that feeling's gone. I can only assume that I was completely mistaken."

I asked what he was mistaken about.

"Mistaken about love at first sight. When you really think about it, there's just no such thing as falling in love. I was wrong all along."

Aha. "So then, Nakagawa, what of your description of being struck dumb at the sight of the angelic light surrounding Nagato? Of being frozen stiff with a single look?"

"I just don't know."

He sounded as apologetic as a meteorologist who'd been asked to give a weather forecast for the next century.

"I just have no idea. I can only guess that it was all in my imagination..."

"I see."

I sounded brusque, but I didn't really mean to attack Nakagawa. Actually, I wasn't that surprised. Things had turned out mostly how I guessed they would. As soon as Nakagawa had made me listen to his mad ravings, I'd wondered if this would be the way of things.

"All right, Nakagawa. I'll pass that on to Nagato. She won't think badly of you. I don't think she was that into the idea to begin with. She'll forget it in an instant."

I heard a sigh of relief through the receiver.

"Okay. I hope so. Please tell her how sorry I am. There must've been something wrong with me."

Most likely, there had been. Nakagawa hadn't had any doubt, but something happened to him. And now, he was back to normal—as though someone had cast a restoration spell on him.

I chatted with Nakagawa for a while, and when his phone card ran low on time, we said our good-byes. We'd probably meet again, eventually.

After hanging up, I called another number.

"Can you meet? Soon?"

I arranged a time and place to meet up with the person on the other end of the call, then picked up my scarf. Shamisen was sprawled out asleep on my coat; he rolled onto the floor and gave me an accusatory glare when I pulled it out from under him.

Yesterday had been difficult, and with all the running around, today had been no better, but soon the day would come to an end.

I rode my bike to that mecca for weirdos, the park in front of the station near Nagato's apartment. This was the place where Nagato had first called me to back in May, as well as the place where I'd first awoken when I traveled back in time with

Asahina to the Tanabata festival three years previous. And more recently, I'd sat here with Asahina the Elder during my second trip back in time. Ah, the memories. They all came flooding back to me.

Sitting on that same old bench waiting for me was a hooded Jawa-like figure. Lit only by the streetlamp, she looked as though she was emerging from the darkness itself.

"Nagato."

I called to the small figure that was looking right at me.

"Sorry for calling you out so suddenly. Just like I told you on the phone, Nakagawa changed his mind."

Nagato stood naturally, then nodded.

"I see."

I looked into her dark eyes.

"Think maybe you could tell me the whole story now?"

I'd ridden over pretty quickly, to keep my body warm. I could withstand the night's chill a little longer.

"I can understand why Nakagawa might have fallen in love with you so quickly. Everyone has a type, after all. But why would he suddenly change his mind today? It's unnatural. And with the football game…it's just too much to swallow that he would get an injury today that just makes him forget about his feelings."

"…"

"You did something. I know I saw you doing something during the game. You were the one who made him have that accident. It was you. Am I right?"

"Yes."

Nagato's answer was simple. She looked up at me.

"I am not the one he saw."

She sounded as though she were reading an essay aloud.

"What he saw was the Data Overmind."

I listened quietly while Nagato continued.

"He has the ability to use me as a terminal to access the Data Overmind."

The cold wind made my ears hurt.

"But I doubt he understood what he was seeing. Mere organic life-forms like humans are on a different level of consciousness than the Data Overmind."

I saw a radiance shining out from behind her . . . light as though from heaven itself. That's how Nakagawa had explained it.

Nagato continued her emotionless explanation.

"What he probably saw was accumulated transcendental knowledge and understanding. While what would have passed through the terminal was insignificant, the information would have overwhelmed him."

So it was a misunderstanding, then. I looked at Nagato's tousled hair and sighed. What Nakagawa was sure had been Nagato's true inner nature had simply been a bit of the Data Overmind. I don't really understand the details, but Nagato's boss possesses a history and a power far beyond the reckoning of any human. It's hardly strange that by accidentally accessing that, Nakagawa got overwhelmed — like a computer freezing when its browser crashes.

"And Nakagawa got confused and thought he'd fallen in love or whatever, then?"

"Yes."

"And then you . . . corrected his feelings?"

The messy bowl-cut hair nodded.

"I analyzed, then deleted, his powers," answered Nagato. "Human intellectual capacity is insufficient for interfacing with the Data Overmind. I projected that eventually he would suffer adverse effects."

I could believe it. One glance at Nagato had been enough to send Nakagawa into a daze, making ten-year plans a few months later. I shuddered to think how crazy he might have gotten if he were left alone.

But there was still one thing I didn't understand.

"Why did Nakagawa even have that power? Has he always had the ability to see the Data Overmind through you?"

"He probably acquired it three years ago."

So it all goes back to that again, eh? The reason Nagato, Asahina, and Koizumi are all here can also be traced back to something that happened three years ago. Or rather, something Haruhi made happen.

That was when I realized it.

The ability Nagato had mentioned—I understood now. Nakagawa might very well have been a candidate to become an esper like Koizumi. Haruhi had definitely done something three years earlier. Something unimaginable, to create a temporal rift, to create an explosion of data, to create espers. So it was entirely possible that Nakagawa could be something like Koizumi. Koizumi's strange statement made sense now. Whether he knew all along or just found out in the last couple of days, he must have known about Nakagawa's power. That's what he meant by "mysterious friends."

"Possibly," agreed Nagato.

Or it might be...I felt a shiver that wasn't just because of the cold. There was no reason that such events were limited to three years ago. Was Haruhi still giving people supernatural abilities? Just like she made cherry blossoms bloom in autumn or turned shrine pigeons into doves? Like that, but with humans?

"..."

Nagato stood and began to walk away, not answering—or perhaps she'd said all she came to say. I stood still as she passed by me, beginning to fade into the darkness like a wandering spirit about to ascend to the Buddha.

"Wait. Can I ask you just one thing?"

I called out to her form, feeling something I couldn't put into words.

Nakagawa had fallen so deeply in love with Nagato that he'd entrusted an incredibly embarrassing love letter to me. To my knowledge, no one else has ever confessed their love to her so directly. What did she think when I read the proposal to her the next day? What did it feel like, hearing someone say, "I love you; I want to spend my life with you," only to find out it was all just a mistake?

The question spilled out of me:

"Were you disappointed?"

In the months since I met her, we've done a lot together. That's true of Haruhi, Asahina, and Koizumi too, but nearly all the incidents involved Nagato somehow, and you could say that she makes my internal pendulum swing the farthest. Haruhi will always get by on her own power. Asahina is fine the way she is, and who cares what happens to Koizumi? But Nagato —

I had to ask. I couldn't help myself.

"When you found out his confession was a mistake, were you a little disappointed?"

"…"

Nagato stopped, then turned her head just enough that I could tell she was looking back. A sudden wind blew her hair across her face.

The night wind was bitterly cold as it sliced over my ears. I waited for a bit, and eventually these small, quiet words were carried to me on the chilly air:

"…Just a bit."

WHERE DID THE CAT GO?

The middle portion of the winter break crept asymptomatically toward the new year; originally we had been looking forward to the mystery that Koizumi and his comrades had set up for us, but the day we arrived at Tsuruya's vacation house, we found ourselves wandering within its daydreamlike interior, and to make matters worse, Nagato collapsed out on the ski slope, which got even Haruhi freaked out.

Fortunately, upon returning to normal dimensionality, Nagato soon recovered, but no matter how you figure it, it was a crazy New Year's Eve Eve—or December thirtieth, as the calendar figures it.

The next day. New Year's Eve.

We had finally come to the brink of a project that had been in the planning stages for some time—the winter version of the mystery game that that overachiever Koizumi had set up when we'd visited a remote island during summer vacation. Of course, this time we knew it was a game, but it was still the main event of this whole excursion. As for the disaster on the snowy mountain;

the phantom villa; the nude, fake Asahina; Euler's theorem (or something); the feverish Nagato fainting—those were all unanticipated and undesired incidents. They weren't Haruhi's style, and I'd like to tell whoever or whatever was responsible that they'll get what's coming to them. Although Nagato was incapacitated, Koizumi and I (it's hard to say how useful Asahina the Younger was) managed somehow. And now in the same villa that housed us, we had Tsuruya as well as Koizumi's associates, none of whom should be underestimated. It would be stranger if something didn't happen.

So.

With the preparations completed, things could now proceed in an SOS Brigade–style—or should I say Haruhi-style—fashion.

I had lingering doubts about whether this was the right way to end the year, but since I was the only one who seemed to hold such doubts, I kept my own counsel.

Just to be clear, the dramatis personae of this episode were: me, Haruhi, Nagato, Asahina, Koizumi, Tsuruya, my little sister, Shamisen the calico cat, Mori, and Arakawa, along with brothers Keiichi and Yutaka Tamaru, who arrived that day.

At Haruhi's urging, Koizumi's Mystery Tour Part Two began.

The morning of New Year's Eve. After polishing off the breakfast that Mori and Arakawa prepared for us, we assembled downstairs in Tsuruya's villa. The first floor was an open common area. The floor consisted of around twenty tatami mats arranged upon a Japanese cedar base, almost like a stage for performing Noh or Kyogen theater. In the middle of the room was a sunken hearth table that could easily seat eight people. The space seemed designed for letting guests relax and make merry to their hearts' content. The floors were also heated, of course, and a quiet heater fan in the corner blew a warm breeze through the room, so both the common area and the hallway were kept effortlessly warm.

Through the windows, the clear blue of the sky above the ski slope was perfectly smooth, as though airbrushed onto a smooth acrylic board—but there would be no snow sports today.

"I'm still a little worried about Yuki, so let's play inside today," said Haruhi, putting a ban on skiing. Of course, Nagato herself had returned to her normal expressionless self, even saying "It's nothing" to try to curtail Haruhi's nursing efforts, but once she'd decided something, Haruhi never reversed herself.

"No! At least stay inside for today. Until I'm sure you're all right, no intense exercise or vigorous activity. Okay?"

Nagato just looked at Haruhi with those big eyes of hers, then looked to the rest of us in turn. I probably wasn't the only one who thought it was almost as if she were saying "I don't mind, but how do you guys feel about it?"

"It would be worrisome to leave Nagato all alone while the rest of us went out. I agree with Haruhi. All of us facing doom in order to save just one…it makes a beautiful story, does it not?" said Koizumi pleasantly.

Tsuruya and my little sister, neither of whom were proper brigade members, also agreed. Shamisen dangled from my sister's arms; his opinion was unclear, but he didn't make any noise, so presumably he had no complaints.

"Shall we push the plan forward, then?" said Koizumi, his gaze pointed out the window. "I had originally planned to start in the evening and end around midnight, but we can begin earlier."

Can't we just begin now? I wondered. Before the light of Haruhi's anticipation burns out my optic nerves?

"Actually, it needs to start snowing again before that can happen. The weather forecast calls for snow showers starting around noon, so we'll need to wait until then."

I had only dragged the heavy Shamisen all the way out here because Koizumi had told me he needed the cat, and now he needed snow? If he needed snow, there were piles of the stuff out-side, I told him.

"I need continuous, ongoing snowfall. I can't explain further—I don't want to ruin the trick."

Having explained, Koizumi smiled to the calico cat in my sister's arms, who was for the moment behaving himself, then picked up a rucksack from next to the heater.

"In anticipation of such a situation, I've brought several games. We can play indoors all day, if need be."

I got a little excited, but then Koizumi started taking analog board games out of his bag. I wondered if he had something against video games.

Sure, we could play, but I was worried about Mori and Arakawa. Arakawa had acted as butler and chef, taking care of everything since our arrival the previous day, and Mori attended to us as a maid—although both of them were really members of the same Haruhi-observing Agency that Koizumi belonged to.

Their demeanor was so servantlike that I felt bad, and I wondered if I should help clean up a little after meals or something.

"No, we're quite all right," the two of them politely assured me. "This is our job, after all."

Huh? Were they actually a butler and a maid? I was pretty sure they were just pretending and were actually part of Koizumi's Agency.

Perhaps having noticed my doubts, Arakawa removed his busi-nesslike mask and smiled. "It's a gift of our occupational train-ing," he said to me.

Thus, neither of them were to be seen in the common area. Perhaps they were busily working away in the kitchen.

As for the other two—Keiichi Tamaru, whose fortune from bio-something or other was large enough to buy himself a private island, and his brother, Yutaka—they wouldn't arrive until around two o'clock, by which time Haruhi had made herself a board-game billionaire, leaving the rest of us bankrupt, and we'd moved on to lunch and Haruhi's nerve-racking punishment games.

The two brothers appeared in the common room where we were all playing, led there by Arakawa.

"The trains were running late because of the snow. We'd planned to be here in the morning."

Keiichi Tamaru looked like a completely normal older guy, and his smile was just as nice as it had been in the summer.

"Hi, guys. It's been a while."

The pleasant Yutaka Tamaru smiled even more brightly than Koizumi as he waved, then spoke to Tsuruya.

"Pleased to meet you—my name is Tamaru. Thank you so much for the invitation. It's an honor to be invited to the Tsuruya family villa."

"Don't worry about it!" said Tsuruya quickly. "You're friends of Koizumi's, and you've put together this game for us, so don't sweat it at all! I love stuff like this!"

No matter whom she was talking to, Tsuruya had a way of making friends in fifteen seconds. I wondered if Asahina's home-room class was like this too. The second-year guys in that class must be pretty happy.

Mori and Arakawa immediately paid their respects. "Welcome, honored guests."

"To think we'd be imposing upon you in the winter too!" said Keiichi with a sheepish smile. "We'll rely upon you, Arakawa."

"Would you care for some lunch?" asked Mori with a small smile.

"No, thank you, we ate on the train," replied Yutaka. "I think we'd like to put our luggage in our room."

"Very good, sir. I'll take it up for you, then." Arakawa politely nodded, then looked to Koizumi.

"Well then, everyone—"

Koizumi stood and addressed the room like a priest conducting a marriage ceremony.

"With everyone assembled, let us begin the game—I should apologize to the Tamaru brothers, who've only just arrived."

Koizumi's smile was a bit forced. Was he unsure whether the game would go smoothly, or did some foolish punch line await us?

"Let me state again that the only victim will be Keiichi. There are no plans for this to become a serial murder case. Also, there is one murderer, and only one. Do not worry about multiple culprits. You need not consider motive. It has no meaning in this game. Finally, I would ask that starting now"—he pointed to a clock on the wall—"from two PM to three PM, no one other than Arakawa and Mori may leave this common area. Yutaka, that goes for you as well. If you need to attend to anything before we begin, please do so now. Is this all understood?"

Everyone nodded.

"It's still seven minutes until two, but that's fine. Shall we begin?" asked Keiichi Tamaru, at which Koizumi nodded.

"Well then."

Reprising his role from this summer as the victim, Keiichi scratched his head, apparently a bit uncomfortable with being the center of attention.

"My room is in the small building, a bit removed from the main house, correct?"

"Yes. I can show you the way," said Mori.

"I think I'll take a bit of a nap. I actually awoke rather early today and am running short on sleep. My nose is acting up, as well—I may have caught a cold."

"Now that you mention it, Keiichi, you are allergic to cats," Yutaka said. "Perhaps that's the trouble."

Even for an act, this was all way too fake.

"That could be it. Uh, please don't worry about me. The allergy's

125

not that severe. It can be rough in a small room, but I'll be fine in a large space like this."

Then, as though to really hammer the point home:

"Please come and wake me around four thirty. Will that be all right — four thirty?"

"Understood, sir."

Mori bowed, then returned to her upright, elegant posture. "This way, please."

Having delivered that series of obviously expository lines, Kei-ichi disappeared into the hallway after Mori. It was all so obvious.

"I'll take my leave, then. Mr. Yutaka, I'll take your luggage."

Arakawa the butler gave a full ninety-degree bow, then quickly gathered up the bag and coat and left.

Having watched the three leave, Koizumi cleared his throat deliberately.

"Well then, that concludes the opening. Please enjoy yourselves in the common area for the next hour."

"Now wait just a minute."

It was Haruhi who objected.

"There's an external building? I don't remember that."

"Sure there is," said Tsuruya. "There's a little place, separate from this house. Didn't you see it?"

"I did not. Koizumi, it's no fair hiding clues. You have to tell us these things. Let's all go take a look at it."

"You were going to see it later anyway..." Koizumi's smile was weak in the face of his already disintegrating plans, but after looking at the clock, he seemed to decide the situation was salvageable. "Understood. There's no harm in doing this much."

"This way!"

Tsuruya walked along, taking the lead. Everyone else followed behind, of course — even my sister, carrying Shamisen, not that one person and one cat were going to be any use in solving the mystery.

Leaving the common area, we came to a hallway that ran parallel to a courtyard. The outside-facing walls were glass, so the garden was plainly visible.

Somewhere along the line it had started to snow.

The accumulated snow was about knee-deep. The garden was totally covered in white, yet somehow I got the sense that it had been done in the Japanese style. In the middle of the courtyard was a small hut.

After a minute's walk, we came to the door that led to the courtyard, which Tsuruya opened. She then pointed.

"That's the place. My grandfather used to use it to meditate. He hated people, see, so whenever he'd come to visit, he'd say something about getting away from my grandma, then lock himself up in there! It's like, if you don't like it, don't come, right? But he'd get ticked off if we didn't invite him. Tough guy to please."

Tsuruya sounded a little nostalgic as she explained.

I tried to notice every little detail. A path led from the main house to the garden shack, but it had no walls—only a roof protected the stone path from snow, even on days that had light snow showers, like today. Things wouldn't go so well if there were a blizzard.

The freezing air gave all of us a chill as it blew through the open door. Shamisen was particularly affected, and he wriggled around, trying to get back to his warm bed. My sister seemed to find this very funny, and before I could stop her, she walked out onto the stone pathway in her slippers, bringing Shamisen closer to a drift of snow.

"Look, Shami, it's snow! Want to taste it?"

Shamisen thrashed around like a bonito on a hook, and as soon as he jumped free of my sister's arms, he expressed his heartfelt irritation with a "meow!" as he disappeared back inside the house. No doubt he was returning to the heated floor to continue his nap.

"Goodness."

Having shown Keiichi to his place, Mori walked back along the stone path with a floating grace. Her smile had an ageless quality to it.

"Is something the matter? If you are looking for Mr. Keiichi, he would be in the shack."

"Are you sure?" asked Haruhi. Her face was already suspicious.

"Quite sure," said Koizumi. "That's what the script says."

Once we'd returned to the common area, the clock pointed to two o'clock on the nose, and Koizumi seemed to sigh in relief.

"I'll say this one more time. Please do not leave this area until after three o'clock. If you absolutely must, please tell me."

Koizumi went over to his rucksack in the corner and took out another item. If there was more, why didn't he just take it all out at once?

"Huh."

Something suddenly occurred to me—Shamisen was nowhere to be seen. Koizumi had left his bag in the corner with the heater, and lately the pillow in front of the heater's vent had been the cat's preferred location. I thought for sure he'd be spitefully sleeping there, but no. Just as I was thinking about it—

"Shall we try this game to pass the time? Suzumiya, will this do?"

My questions were erased by Koizumi speaking.

"Sure," said Haruhi, sounding somehow pleased with herself. "It might be a little early, but we'll wind up playing anyway, so we might as well. Gimme that, Koizumi."

Koizumi handed over the bag, whereupon Haruhi took something curious out of it—some sheets of paper with pictures drawn on them, along with a corresponding number of envelopes. She spread them out on the hearth table around which we all sat. I was suddenly filled with a sense of nostalgia.

"It's fukuwarai!" said Haruhi. "You played it when you were a kid, right? Just pin the eyes, noses, and mouths on blank faces while blindfolded. I'd planned to play tomorrow, but we've got time, so let's do it now. Plus, this isn't just any old fukuwarai."

That much was obvious. Just looking at the facial outlines and hairstyles, it was clear that they were caricatures of our faces. They were drawn well enough that even without eyes or noses, you could still tell who was who. I could see why Haruhi was so proud of them.

"I drew these. They're handmade! There's even one for Tsuruya. And I knew Kyon's little sister was coming, so I made one for her too. Oh—sorry, Yutaka. I couldn't really remember your face."

"Oh, don't worry," said Yutaka easily. "That's probably for the best, really."

"Probably!"

Haruhi grinned and looked over the brigade members.

"Ready? We're gonna play with our own faces. And no do-overs! When the faces are done, we're gonna glue them in place and hang them on the clubroom wall, so be serious. If you don't, you'll be stuck with a weirdo version of your face in our clubroom forever!"

Her thinking was something else. She'd done an amazing job of capturing everybody's features. If we managed to line them up right, they really would look like cartoon versions of us. Based on that alone, we'd want to be serious about it.

Still, when had she found the time to do all this?

"All right, who's going first?" asked Haruhi.

Tsuruya's hand shot up energetically; hers was the only one.

While Tsuruya was a force to be reckoned with, even she didn't have X-ray vision. Blindfolded with a towel, she made a hilarious arrangement of her own features that caused the table to burst into laughter, and when she herself saw the completed portrait, she rolled over and nearly died. Not even a laugh bag could be so funny.

Next up was Koizumi, whose clever, handsome features were totally ruined. When the blindfold was removed and he saw the results of his work, he made a disappointed face—but I couldn't really laugh, since my turn was up next.

I'd never felt so nervous playing fukuwarai. Just as I was psyching myself up for it—

"Excuse me for a moment," Koizumi muttered to me. "I need to go speak to Arakawa et al about tomorrow's arrangements."

And with that, he left the common area. I didn't know what he needed to meet with them about, but that wasn't my problem at the moment. The fate of my clubroom portrait was in the hands of my own sense of spatial orientation.

My round of fukuwarai ended with a burst of laughter. Oh well. It would've spoiled the mood if I'd arranged a perfect face, I suppose. Hey—Tsuruya, you're laughing a little too hard, I thought.

As I took off the towel amid Tsuruya's and Haruhi's cackling, I saw Koizumi return. Reflexively, I checked the clock.

It was just past two thirty.

"Pardon my absence."

For some reason, Koizumi had gone somewhere and returned carrying Shamisen. What was he doing with that cat? I asked him.

"Ah, nothing. He was just following Mori around too much in the kitchen."

Koizumi set the calico down on the cushion in front of the heater, whereupon the cat curled up in front of the warm airflow. Putting a well-fed cat somewhere warm is the best way to get it to behave.

"How did you do?"

Koizumi sat down next to me at the table and took a look at

the proceedings. My little sister had inflicted her paste upon the portraits of myself, Tsuruya, and Koizumi. Surely there was something better than these to decorate the clubroom with—Asahina's cosplay photos, for example.

Time passed, and the game of fukuwarai proceeded with Asahina, then Nagato. Asahina's hands were charmingly hesitant as she felt around for the parts of her face, and in the end her portrait was just as charming. Nagato then completed a surrealist version of herself that absolutely slew Tsuruya. Nagato regarded her own work curiously, having no idea what was so funny about it.

As we continued to play—

"Excuse me, everyone—it will soon be three o'clock."

Koizumi made his announcement.

"I'd like everyone to take a short break. I'll need you all to stay here from three to four o'clock, so if you need to use the bathroom, now is your chance."

Everyone left the room except Nagato, Yutaka, Koizumi, and me. Nagato continued to regard her fukuwarai portrait, while Yutaka watched her profile, seemingly amused.

I turned to Koizumi.

"When will the murder happen?"

"More important, take a look outside the window." Koizumi pointed outside. "You can see that it is snowing, correct? Please remember that. If it hadn't been snowing, I would have had to ask you to pretend that it was, but fortunately, things are working out nicely."

As I was scrutinizing Koizumi's easy smile, the four girls returned. Yutaka seemed like the most likely suspect to me. He had no other role to play, after all. Not that he was actually doing anything suspicious at the moment.

Haruhi sat back down at the hearth.

"Koizumi, let's do that next. Get it out for me, will you?"

"Understood. That game, yes?"

Koizumi again went over to his rucksack. Wondering what handmade nonsense he was going to pull out this time, I followed him over. He rummaged around for a moment, then, looking back at me, produced a large sheet of paper by some sleight of hand.

"Please give this to Suzumiya."

Koizumi handed me a large sheet of paper that was folded over onto itself; it fluttered slightly in the heater's breeze. As I tried to open it, I felt suddenly uneasy. It wasn't because of the big sheet of paper. There was Koizumi right in front of me, his hand on his bag, and next to it was the heater. Also there was Shamisen, sleeping comfortably away on the cushion.

There wasn't anything strange about it, and yet something was off. Had Koizumi seemed nervous when I'd gotten close to him?

"Kyon, what're you doing? Bring it over here!"

I reluctantly brought the mysterious sheet of paper back to the table, Koizumi following me.

The clock indicated exactly three o'clock.

"Koizumi and I made it!"

Haruhi's pride seemed to hit a crescendo. It was written all over her face.

"It's a board game just for the SOS Brigade! I drew every square by hand, so you'd better be grateful."

Incidentally, the first square my piece landed on said this:

KYON ONLY — THIRTY PUSH-UPS.

Other squares said things like PLAY STRIP ROCK-PAPER-SCISSORS WITH THE NEXT PERSON WHO STOPS, or SAY FIVE NICE THINGS TO THE CHIEF, or ANSWER EVERYBODY'S QUESTIONS HONESTLY (AND EVERYBODY HAS TO ASK THE MOST EMBARRASSING QUESTIONS THEY CAN), and so on. It was a board game filled with Haruhi-style punishments.

After much fuss, obviously we wound up playing it. Asahina and Yutaka landed on the strip rock-paper-scissors square, but Asahina's blank face made it clear she didn't have the slightest idea what the terms meant, so I wound up playing in her stead. What followed was a parade of squares I can only assume were designed to exhaust me. An hour later, when Tsuruya finally reached the goal, I was about ready to collapse.

I'm sure Koizumi didn't care about me a bit, but he raised his hand and spoke, as though he'd been looking forward to it.

"Your attention please, everybody. It is now four o'clock," he announced like a timekeeper for a live broadcast. "It is now free time. Please assemble back here by four thirty. Also, if possible, please refrain from going outside. Of course, that only applies if you are not the murderer."

"Well then, if you'll excuse me," said Yutaka Tamaru, smiling meaningfully as he stood. "I need to unpack the luggage in my room. Don't worry, I'll be back in five minutes."

He left immediately thereafter, whereupon Haruhi announced, "I'm going to the kitchen," and she did, taking Tsuruya with her, returning a few moments later bearing tea cakes and drinks. No one else left the table. Nobody wanted to be accused of being the murderer, after all—especially if it wasn't true.

Incidentally, I should add that Yutaka did indeed return five minutes later.

It was just past four thirty in the afternoon.

Mori entered the common area and made an announcement.

"Mr. Keiichi is not answering the door."

She pretended to look unsettled.

"I checked the shack, but there is no response, and the door has been locked."

"It's time!" Haruhi said, standing up gallantly. "We'll need to check the scene of the crime first."

Every inch the tour guide, Koizumi headed down the hallway, the rest of us trailing behind.

Upon opening the doors that led to the courtyard, we found outdoor shoes set out for us in advance. After putting them on and making our way down the path to the shack, we found Arakawa waiting beside the door.

"What's the situation?" asked Haruhi.

"Just as Mori said, I'm sure. The door is locked from the inside, and Mr. Keiichi is the only one who has the key. Incidentally, there are no duplicates."

"That's how things are," noted Koizumi. "However, there is no need to break the door down. Please simply assume that there are no duplicate keys. Arakawa, the key, please."

Arakawa the butler extended his hand, which contained a key.

"This key does not really exist. Please act as though that were true."

Koizumi opened the door, through which Haruhi immediately strode.

"Hi."

Keiichi waved at us. Lying next to the futon, the elder Tamaru brother pointed to his chest.

"I've been stabbed again."

A knife handle stuck out of his chest—a gag toy I'd seen before.

"Who stabbed you?" asked Haruhi.

"I can't say. I'm dead, after all, and corpses don't talk."

With that, his hand flopped down onto the floor.

"Everyone, please," began Koizumi, "take a careful look around the room. The key to the shack is here on the desk. This is, of course, the one that Keiichi brought with him. That means that the murderer did not leave through the door."

Koizumi approached the window that faced the veranda.

"The window is closed, but it is not locked, which means that the killer escaped through it. Also, snow is piling up outside."

Once Koizumi opened the window, we all peered out at the courtyard.

"Allow me to explain the killer's escape route. We know that he or she did not leave through the door, but escaped through the window. While walking through the snow would of course leave footprints behind, none are visible. Look above the window—the eaves of this shack overhang all four corners, and directly beneath them, the layer of snow is very thin. The killer walked along the outside wall to get to the path that returns to the house."

I looked down at the ground that Koizumi was pointing to, then back up to the sky. Snow was slowly falling.

"The falling snow has covered up the killer's footprints. Based on this rate of snowfall…the footprints wouldn't have disappeared in less than thirty minutes."

Then, as if to confirm that everybody understood, he added, "This is the scenario. I ask for your cooperation. The corpse cannot talk, but as the game's master, I will not deceive you."

"Hmm."

Haruhi looked back and forth from the snow to Koizumi, then frowned and folded her arms.

"Is that all?"

Koizumi only pointed to the futon. Something seemed to be moving around beneath the soft comforter. Could it be—?

It was Haruhi who pulled the comforter aside, to reveal—

"Shamisen?"

It was definitely our cat, narrowing his eyes at the sudden light.

We returned to the common area and sat around the table.

Mori and Arakawa quietly stood back, while Keiichi—his corpse duties concluded—was probably enjoying a nice cup of coffee somewhere.

"Let's put the facts in order. Keiichi entered the shack at exactly two o'clock. His body was discovered just a moment ago, at four thirty. We know for sure that the crime was committed some-time during those two and a half hours. The doors were locked from the inside, and the key was inside the room. Let me reiterate that you must assume that there were no duplicate keys. The window that faced the veranda was unlocked, which means the killer escaped through that window."

Koizumi explained the facts.

"It would be impossible to reach the path to the shack from the window without leaving footprints. The fact that there are no footprints means that the prints that were once there have been covered by the falling snow."

He looked at the calico cat that my sister held.

"Moreover, Shamisen was present at the scene of the crime when the corpse was discovered. Now, let's think back. Before discovering him with the body, when did we last see the cat?"

I'd seen him right after Koizumi told everyone to take a bath-room break. He'd been sleeping by the rucksack when Koizumi took Haruhi's punishment board game out of it, I told everyone.

"What? Really?"

Haruhi pushed on her forehead with her finger.

"Now that you mention it, I don't have any memory of seeing the cat for the last three hours. Was he really there?"

"I think he was there…" said Asahina without much confi-dence. "I, um, saw him a few times when we were playing fuku-warai. He was sleeping on the cushion."

"That was the last I saw of him too!" said Tsuruya. "Right when I stood up to head to the bathroom, I saw the kitty cat all curled up there. I think he was there when we were board-gamin' it up too."

It seemed that based on witness testimony, I was the last one to have seen him. Which meant that Shamisen had no alibi from three to four o'clock.

Sometime during the time we were absorbed with the game,

he'd woken up and wandered off somewhere. Eventually he'd found his way into Keiichi's room, then snuck into the futon...

Wait—that can't be right.

"There's no way the cat would decide to go into the shack of his own volition," I said. "He hated the cold so much he freaked out just by being outside for a bit. He flinched away from the snow, and he couldn't have opened the door from the main house to the courtyard by himself."

"True."

Koizumi voiced his mild agreement.

"It stands to reason that someone must have taken him there. Either Keiichi or the killer."

"Well, it couldn't have been Keiichi."

Haruhi butted in.

"He said he was allergic to cats. That was foreshadowing, although it was kinda fake."

"Of course, that was part of the setup for the mystery. It would have been a bit problematic otherwise. So whoever brought the cat into the room must be the killer. This seems to be a hint."

Haruhi raised her hand at Koizumi's declaration.

"Now wait just a minute. So that means Shamisen was with us until three, whereupon he went missing. The killer had to leave the shack no later than four thirty. It took half an hour for the snow to cover the tracks, so that narrows it down to four. That means that the killer took Shamisen—and killed Keiichi—sometime between three and four."

That sounded right, I said.

"The hell it does!" Haruhi said. "Something's wrong. The only ones who left the room at four were Tsuruya, Yutaka, and me. But I was with Tsuruya the whole time, so that means she's not the killer. Yutaka's suspicious, but if it took at least half an hour for the snow to cover the tracks, he couldn't have done it either."

Good point, I said.

"It's no point at all! It means everyone here has an alibi! We were all here during that hour."

Eight of us played the board game starting at three—Haruhi, Asahina, Nagato, Koizumi, my little sister, Tsuruya, Yutaka Tamaru, and me. Since the break at three until the beginning of free activity time at four, not a single one of us had left the common area—except for the cat.

"Could it have been Arakawa or Mori?" Haruhi wondered.

The two servants were immediately brought in for interrogation. Haruhi sounded like a police detective as she questioned them.

"Well then, Mr. Arakawa, let's hear your alibi, starting from three o'clock."

Arakawa the butler gave a polite bow.

"I've been in the kitchen since two o'clock, cleaning up after lunch and preparing for tonight's dinner and tomorrow's breakfast."

"Do you have anyone who will vouch for that?"

"If I may," said Mori, her smile as pure as her maid uniform, "I was with Mr. Arakawa the entire time, helping him prepare. He didn't leave my sight until I went to wake up Mr. Keiichi."

"Likewise," said Arakawa. "At the very least, I can state with confidence that Miss Mori did not leave the kitchen between three and four o'clock."

"Which means you're testimony for each other."

Haruhi nodded thoughtfully.

"But that means you could have conspired to commit the crime together—or that one of you is covering for the other. Am I wrong?"

Haruhi's shining eyes turned to Koizumi, seeking an explanation.

"That is not the case. This mystery is predicated on a single perpetrator, and neither Arakawa nor Mori will give false testimony. I'll just come right out and say it—neither of these two is the killer," said Koizumi.

"Well, then who is it?" said Haruhi happily. "Everyone's alibi is perfect, which means none of us could have killed Keiichi!"

Koizumi seemed slightly pleased. Haruhi seemed to have hit upon the point he wanted her to hit. With a smile, he replied:

"That is precisely what I want you to think about and solve. There'd be no game otherwise."

"The first thing we need to think about is why the killer needed Shamisen."

Having appointed herself chair of the investigation, Haruhi poked at the nose of the calico cat my sister held.

"Otherwise, what's the point? What was the killer doing that they needed a cat for?"

If the stupid cat would just talk, he could've provided crucial testimony—he was a witness, after all.

"What I think is that the killer needed Shamisen to be there for some reason," said Haruhi.

Even I knew that much. The question was, what was that reason?

"Kitty, kitty cat...hmm..." Asahina muttered charmingly under her breath, her hand touching her chin as she mulled it over. "Cat. Calico cat. Calico. Hmm...kitty...kitty food..."

She didn't seem to be getting anywhere, though.

Tsuruya always seemed to have pretty sharp eyes; she stuck out her tongue and rolled her eyes back as she thought. I guessed that was just how she looked when she was thinking hard. She silently folded her arms, maintaining her funny expression.

Speaking of silence, there was Nagato. Although at the moment, it was probably best for her to stay silent. I'd bet with a fair amount of confidence that Nagato had seen through whatever trick Koizumi was playing. Maybe I'd get her to tell us who the culprit was once everyone else had given up, I thought.

"Shamisen's alibi is the key. If only he hadn't shown himself the whole time...a locked room trick? A locked room using snow to impose a time limit...hmm?"

Muttering to herself, Haruhi suddenly looked up. She regarded Koizumi's smile, then Yutaka's calm expression, then Shamisen's sleepy face.

"Time limit...alibi...oh, I see!"

Haruhi suddenly turned to me.

"Kyon, what do you think of when you hear the word 'alibi'?"

"Cop shows," I answered immediately, then regretted it. "Uh... made-for-TV suspense movies," I tried again, then regretted it even more. Time continued to pass as I tried to think of what to say next.

"He's a decoy!" Haruhi answered her own question. "Of course he's a decoy! Shamisen's being used to trick us!"

Trick us how? I asked.

"Just think about it. Here—when does Shamisen's alibi get vague?"

From three to four thirty. I was the last one to see him before he teleported to the scene of the murder.

"Forget about that time period. Think about what happened earlier."

Before three? Hadn't we just been wandering around the villa then? No—wait.

"Koizumi, when was it that you carried the cat back to the common area?"

I thought I noticed Koizumi's handsome smile turn slightly more angular.

"Just a bit past two thirty," he said.

"And where did you bring him from?"

"The kitchen." Koizumi smiled at Mori. "Isn't that right?"

"Yes."

Mori looked to Shamisen with a smile.

"Just as I was tidying up, the cat came in and started sashaying around at my feet. I gave in and let him have some table scraps, but he only seemed to become more persistent. So when Mr. Koizumi passed through, he took the cat with him."

I remembered Koizumi saying something about making plans for tomorrow and leaving his seat.

"And that was at two thirty?"

In response to my question, the plainly dressed maid gave me a smile so elegant I almost flinched away.

"Yes . . . yes, it was. I didn't check the time, so I can't be perfectly accurate, but I think it was around that time."

"And when did Shamisen start hanging around you?"

"At two o'clock, when I returned from the shack, he was grooming himself in the kitchen."

So that much matched up. Our calico cat had roamed around the villa after escaping my younger sister's clutches, had begged for food from Mori, then around two thirty had been carried by Koizumi back into the common room, where he'd commenced napping on the cushion in front of the heater.

"So he has an alibi from two to three."

There was an explanation for his movements for that hour. But what had Shamisen seen between then and when he went to the shack? I wondered.

"That's where the trick is."

Haruhi narrowed her eyes and stroked her throat. Then, as if something had jumped out at her —

"All we know for sure is that one hour. The rest is still vague, especially where he went and what he did after three. The cat's alibi, and when he fell into the hands of the killer . . ."

Haruhi frowned, deep in thought; I went ahead and frowned too. My sister looked up at me with a puzzled expression, while Yutaka only smiled and said nothing. He probably knew the truth, being the prime suspect.

"Shall I give you a hint?"

"No, wait."

I cut off Koizumi and thought.

It was around two o'clock when Keiichi had gone to the shack.

The cat was last seen at three, and nobody had seen him again until we found him with Keiichi's corpse at four thirty.

If the killer had exited the shack through the window, it had to be with enough time for the falling snow to cover his or her tracks, so the murder had happened between three and four.

But between three and four, all of us—including Yutaka—were in the open common area, and none of us left. Only at four did Yutaka, Haruhi, and Tsuruya leave.

All right. I nodded, satisfied.

"I give up. Give me a hint."

Koizumi shrugged.

"I would have thought that the first to notice would be either you or your sister," was all he said before clamming up again.

"Huh?"

What kind of hint was that? I couldn't imagine that my sister was sharper than Tsuruya or Haruhi.

"Oh, I see!" Haruhi shouted.

Tsuruya's bright voice rang out immediately after Haruhi's.

"That's it, Haru-meow! The cat's alibi is the same as the killer's!" she said, the realization all over her face. "Yes, yes! That's it! That's why the cat had to be here! Not just anywhere, here! Not in the shack, but in the room with everyone else!"

I didn't have the slightest idea what she was saying. Asahina and I were dumbstruck, but Haruhi seemed to understand, and her voice rose accordingly.

"Right! Nice one, Tsuruya! For that hour, the cat had to be in a place where everyone could see it, because otherwise, the killer's own alibi would be blown!"

"Bingo!"

Tsuruya snapped her fingers.

"Shami didn't go missing at three, but at two thirty! He has two hours without an alibi, not just an hour and a half!"

"Which pushes the time of the murder forward half an hour,

from between two thirty to four ... no, sometime in the half hour between two thirty and three—basically, the true crime happened at two thirty. Right?"

"Right!"

I told them to hold up. The two energetic girls sounded like they were closing in on the truth, but what about the rest of us? I had no clue what they were going on about.

"You're so slow, Kyon. Who would be confused by the fact that Shamisen went missing from three to four thirty, then was found at the crime scene?"

Uh, us, right?

"Okay, and who stands to gain from that?"

Nobody? I asked.

"It's not nobody! The killer took Shamisen off and locked him in the room. The fact that they did that meant they needed to do that. What part of that did they need?"

Haruhi's eyes bored into me accusingly, as though she were the true killer, glaring at a detective.

"Uh," I said. "The fact that Shamisen was there means that ... the killer took him there, so the moment when Shamisen disappeared is the time of the murder, so ..."

"That's right."

What's right? I wanted to know.

"What do you mean, 'what'? That's what everybody would think. That's the trick! The killer needs us to be thinking about the time when Shamisen doesn't have an alibi."

"Everybody has an alibi from three to four," said Tsuruya. "But what about starting at two o'clock? We were told not to leave the room, and we didn't, right?"

"That's because the killer needed to preserve their alibi between two and three," said Haruhi. "So they had to make it seem like Shamisen was still here. Why? Because Shamisen going missing from three to four thirty would actually establish their own alibi.

Shamisen couldn't be both here and at the scene of the crime at the same time. If the cat is here, we assume that the killer hasn't yet taken him to the shack. But you were the last person to see Shamisen, and that was around three o'clock. Making us think that the killer had to have taken Shamisen to the shack sometime after three is obviously the trick!"

"Which means there's only one person who could possibly be the killer! It's the person whose alibi around two thirty is shaky, and the person who was closest to the cat at three!"

Tsuruya giggled happily.

"Kyon, don't you see? Think about it this way. We just need to find the person who had the opportunity to kill Keiichi between two o'clock, when he shut himself in the shack, and four, when we broke in. Turns out it's impossible for everybody except one person! Except that if we narrow it down to three o'clock, that person also has an alibi. So what we've gotten wrong is the time of the murder!"

Not to be beaten, Haruhi grinned.

"Right, right! Keiichi was killed before three, and that's when Shamisen was taken to the shack."

"Now wait just a second," I said. "How do you explain that I saw Shamisen at three? And what about Asahina seeing him sleeping a bit before three? Don't tell me he split himself."

"You still don't get it?"

Haruhi's smile was full of pride.

"Let me explain what the killer did. Neither Mori nor Arakawa is the killer, and we don't have to doubt their testimony. Since the game master gave them the stamp of approval, we'll ignore them."

Apparently the only ones who hadn't figured it out were me, Asahina, and my sister.

Haruhi looked us over, then started explaining victoriously.

"The killer left the common area sometime between two and three and took Shamisen out of the kitchen. He or she then took Shamisen to the shack where Keiichi was. It doesn't matter whether it was locked or not—either way, the killer entered the room and stabbed Keiichi. Then he or she locked the room from inside, left Shamisen there, exited the room via the window, moved around to the path, then returned to the house—empty-handed, of course."

"Hang on," I said. "What about the fact that I saw Shamisen at three? He was sleeping on the cushion in front of the heater."

"That wasn't Shamisen!"

Haruhi glanced at Tsuruya, and after having confirmed that Tsuruya's expression indicated agreement, she continued.

"It's the logical conclusion. There's only one killer, and the only time that killer could have acted alone was during a few minutes around two thirty, while moving easily between the main house and the shack was impossible for everybody else, no matter what time it was. Regardless of his or her alibi, that person is the killer. And what do we need to destroy that alibi? Don't you see? You just need to show that Shamisen went missing around two thirty. Which means the only explanation for the Shamisen you saw was that it was a fake."

Tsuruya butted in.

"So lemme just ask you, Kyon. The Shamisen you saw between two thirty and three—was that the real Shamisen?"

When she put it that way, I didn't have an answer. I only saw the cat from behind—both when it was picked up and when it was sleeping on the cushion. That was all I saw.

But a fake? What kind of fake? Was she saying that Shamisen had been secretly cloned somewhere along the line? I asked.

"Who knows?" answered Haruhi calmly. "I told you, it's the logical conclusion. The cat you saw on that cushion between two thirty and three was not Shamisen. It couldn't have been Shamisen. I don't know if it was a clone, or a doll, or just a look-alike. All I know is that it wasn't your calico."

"Hey, Haru-meow, I think everybody's figured it out, so let's just say the name of the killer, 'kay? We're not gonna get any-where otherwise," said Tsuruya excitedly, at which Haruhi nodded.

"Good point. If we wait for Kyon, he'll be thinking about it all winter break at this rate. Together, then?"

"Gotcha. The killer is—"

The two girls smiled together at a certain individual, then with double-barreled synchronization, shouted out the name of the killer.

"—Koizumi!"

Koizumi raised both hands, like a suspect run down by two famous bounty hunters holding Winchester rifles.

"Right you are," he said, his bitter smile looking a bit defeated. "I was the killer. I had hoped you would take a bit more time to think it through, but Suzumiya and Tsuruya were too sharp."

Haruhi's mouth bent into a smile.

"Why didn't you give us free time starting at three, instead of four? It would've taken more time to pin down the culprit, I think."

"That would have indeed made ascertaining the killer more dif-ficult," Koizumi explained. "If any one of you had left for more than five minutes starting at three o'clock—that's the amount of time it takes to get from the house to the shack and back—and had been alone for that time, that would've made it impossible to exclude you from the list of suspects. In other words, there would be no way for you to plausibly deny being the killer, so I decided it would be better to remove everybody from being a suspect. The game would have been too difficult otherwise."

That made sense, but I wondered if he hadn't just thought of it.

"Where did you hide the body double for Shamisen?"

"In my room. I had Arakawa bring it there before the game began. That doesn't make him an accessory—from the perspec-tive of the story, I brought it in myself."

With an expression like a day laborer reaching the end of his shift, Koizumi continued.

"After the murder, before returning here, I went and got the double out of my room. The rest, you've figured out."

So that was the cat Koizumi had carried in a bit after two thirty. Still—

"So where's the cat?" I asked again. "Where'd the fake go? It still hasn't shown up, not since I spotted it last. Don't tell me you were able to make it disappear again."

The defeated Koizumi looked to Haruhi, whereupon our gallant brigade chief marched over to the heater in the corner of the room.

"Kyon, think back carefully now. Koizumi was next to the calico cat you saw sleeping on the cushion, right? You took the board game from him and then came back to the table, and we were all paying attention to you. Koizumi took the chance to stick the sleeping cat into his rucksack. So—"

Standing by the wall, Haruhi picked up the rucksack that was sitting next to the heater vent.

"—that's where it still is."

She tipped over the bag, and sure enough, a big ball of fur came tumbling out.

"Shamisen?"

I blurted out the name despite myself; the cat really did look like Shamisen. It was a perfect copycat, down to the body shape and pattern—save one big difference: it was female. Male calicos are incredibly rare, and if you want to know why, I suggest asking your biology teacher.

The fake Shamisen sat dazedly on the floor for a moment, then eventually flicked her tail and walked over to my sister and sniffed noses with the real Shamisen, whom my sister was holding. My cat stared round-eyed at the female, then escaped my sister's clutches and sniffed the female's tail. The two circled around in pursuit of each other's tails, which ended about ten seconds later when Shamisen took a swipe at the female.

"Hey! Bad Shami!"

My sister scooped up the growling Shamisen, whereupon the female calico looked around, then for some reason decided to occupy Nagato's lap.

"..."

Nagato looked blankly down, meeting the gaze of the cat that looked up at her with a demand in her eyes. Eventually, Nagato extended a hesitant hand.

Satisfied with Nagato's timid petting, the impostor kitty curled up and closed her eyes. She certainly did resemble Shamisen, but there were differences. I'd lived with Shamisen for two months—more than enough time to tell the face of my own household's cat from some other animal.

"Ah, so that's why you said you thought my sister or I would have noticed first."

"Yes. When you got close, I was breaking out in a cold sweat. If you'd actually noticed, I was planning to whisper into your ear to play along. But based on your expression, you didn't seem to have noticed at all."

Sorry, pal, I mentally apologized to Shamisen.

"The hardest part of all of this was finding that cat."

What follows is Master Koizumi's supplemental explanation.

"As far as cats identical to Shamisen go, when I started looking I had no luck finding one. I had naively thought that all calicos were equal—how wrong I was. After skipping all over the country, I finally found a stray with similar coloration, though not quite exact. Ultimately parts of her fur had to be dyed. But even that wasn't enough. She also had to be trained."

What kind of training? I asked.

"She had to learn 'wait,' like a dog. If she started wandering around, that would ruin everything, so I had to teach her to sit still and feign sleep until she got a sign from me. If she moved or meowed during the half hour on the cushion, then during the hour and a half inside my rucksack, the trick wouldn't have worked."

Koizumi shook his head, thinking about it. If the cat had actually learned that kind of trick, it might have a future in showbiz—and showbiz would be even easier for the guy who'd learned how to hypnotize cats.

"I named her Shamisen the Second, Shami Two for short. I couldn't think of anything else."

Having given that strange excuse, Koizumi cleared his throat.

"So, our mystery game has come to an end. I trust no one will mind awarding both Suzumiya and Tsuruya the prize for correctly solving the mystery—said prize will be presented in a moment."

Koizumi bowed slowly.

"This concludes the day's entertainment. I thank everyone for their cooperation, particularly Tsuruya for the use of her family's villa, Keiichi Tamaru for playing the role of the victim, Yutaka for acting solely as a misdirection, and Arakawa and Mori for all their help. Thank you all for your support."

Haruhi and Tsuruya started clapping like monkeys, followed by my sister, then the baffled Asahina. Seeing even Nagato clapping quietly, Shami Two still in her lap, I wound up applauding as well.

Good job, Koizumi.

The prize was a small electroplated trophy. It was decorated with a stylized cat that actually looked a bit like Shamisen doing a headstand. Haruhi and Tsuruya held it up, their fingers flashing V-for-victory poses, so I gave up and snapped a picture—with Shamisens One and Two, of course.

Later, Arakawa brought out the traditional New Year's Eve soba noodles a little early. Haruhi and Tsuruya immediately grabbed their chopsticks and went crazy, while Koizumi's chopsticks barely twitched. Now that I thought about it, I'd never seen him really tear into a meal.

"So, how did you like the game?"

Well now, this was a rare thing indeed. Even in the house of illusions the previous day, Koizumi hadn't shown me the slightly uneasy smile he now wore. I didn't really feel like complimenting the scenario, but...

"I guess it was all right," I said.

I gulped down some onions in noodle broth.

"Haruhi's mood is as good as ever. Aren't you satisfied?"

"That's good, if true. It means this was worth arranging—it was all for her amusement, after all."

There was that—it'd been nothing but a pain for me, and I couldn't say I felt particularly resolved. Asahina didn't seem to have understood either, and she was busily drawing lines in a memo pad.

"This is two o'clock, and this is three, and the cat was here from two to three...wait, no, half an hour? Huh? Kitty, kitty..."

Asahina muttered away, slurping up her noodles with a confused-looking face. The person who understood the least was my sister; she hadn't heard a single thing, but there she sat, happily stirring up the contents of her bowl.

I breathed a sigh of relief to see Nagato's appetite returning to normal, with the female calico still in her lap. Basically, it was good to see everybody acting like themselves, save Koizumi, who seemed to be trying to elicit sympathy.

"I've been totally preoccupied by the planning for this ever since the winter field trip was announced. Thanks to everyone, I'm finally free. I don't think I'm really cut out to be the killer or mastermind type. I'm happy to leave the detective role to others too. I think being a commentator suits me best."

If it were up to me, I'd have the commentator role abolished— I didn't want any more crazy things happening that needed commentary. Just as I was making that wish, an idea flashed through my mind.

"For the next murder mystery, why bother doing a whole performance? If it's all planned, wouldn't it be easier to just hand out booklets with the script?"

Koizumi made a face like noodles were stuck in his throat, then spoke like a boxer, bleeding because of an accidental head-butt and being told by the doctor to forfeit.

"...That's a good point," he said unwillingly.

"So hey, Koizumi—"

Haruhi spoke up as she got a refill on her noodles from Mori.

"We're leaving next summer's event to you! We've done an island and a snowy mountain, so next we'll need someplace even weirder. Like someplace with a weird name! Someplace overseas might be good. Yeah, like a castle! An old stone castle would be perfect!"

Haruhi destroyed my dreams and Koizumi's as she whipped her chopsticks around like a baton.

"I know the perfect place—my dad's friend owns a castle overseas!"

Tsuruya joined in, unfortunately, and seemed even more excited than Haruhi.

"Hey, guys, did you hear that? Get your passports ready for summer!"

Koizumi and I exchanged a glance and a sigh, proof that neither of us had the strength to withstand the tag-teaming of Haruhi and Tsuruya. I was just the guy who was going to try to get Haruhi to give up on her overseas travel plans, and Koizumi was the SOS Brigade's drama producer of last resort. The way things were ending up, battling unseen opponents was starting to sound pretty good.

If I didn't do something, we'd wind up opening an overseas

branch of the SOS Brigade. I really didn't want things to get too out of hand, or so I told myself as eloquently as I could.

This was probably the first New Year's Eve I'd ever passed without a single glance at the television.

We played another round of Haruhi's board game, this time including Mori and the others. As Haruhi had fun and I got worn out, the luxurious dinner and evening conversation came to an end, and eventually we realized that the hour was getting late.

"Once we wake up tomorrow, we can write our New Year's resolutions and play hanetsuki in the snow!" Haruhi shouted.

Hey, at least let us eat some zouni first before we go play badminton in the snow, I thought.

"It'll be the new year, after all, so we gotta do the basics. Although we already played fukuwarai and my board game a little early."

Haruhi looked at the wall clock as she continued.

"It'll be bad if we don't do the first shrine visit of the year too."

I didn't think it would be particularly bad. I didn't care how generous the gods and Buddhas were; I doubted they really wanted Haruhi coming around their temples. The shrine where we did our location shooting was probably sending out letters saying we were banned from entering ever again, I told her.

"What're you talking about? We're lucky enough to live in a country that mixes up all kinds of religions, so it'd be a waste not to do everything! Celebrating Christmas without doing New Year's would be like ordering a gourmet meal and then leaving after just looking at the utensils! We can't miss doing the first shrine visit!"

Well, in that case, why not just build a snow temple out in the yard and stick an offering box in front of it? Of course, we'd dress up Asahina as a shrine maiden and put her inside the temple.

That way we wouldn't have to slog all the way to some existing shrine, and for my part I'd pray there day and night. Eventually word would get around, and we'd get people making the pilgrimage to see her all the time—and I promise the donation box wouldn't run empty, I said.

"Idiot!"

Haruhi clung to Asahina's shoulder.

"Although it's hard to give up on the idea of shrine maidens, I want to see Mikuru in a full kimono! We'll do shrine maidens after we get back from the trip. We'll find some temple or shrine to go to. Oh, obviously Yuki has to dress up too—and so will I!"

Once Asahina's earlobe turned red from her nibbling, Haruhi checked the time again.

"Hey, everybody, it's time!"

At Haruhi's direction, we all sat in a circle, kneeling down in the traditional way. In addition to the five SOS Brigade members, Tsuruya was also part of the circle, and next to her sat my sister and the two cats. Also, the bonus quartet of the Tamaru brothers, the butler, and the maid joined us at Haruhi's behest. Were they really all right with that? I wondered. If things went badly, they'd wind up getting ordered around like brigade members.

But my worries aside, everyone was smiling their own unique smiles. And why not? Show me a guy who's frowning on a day like this, and I'll show you a guy who doesn't have a calendar. I couldn't think of a reason to complain.

When Haruhi gave the signal, we all bowed and said the standard Happy New Year phrase: *omedetou gozaimasu.*

It's old and boring, but if we changed it, we'd surely miss that phrase.

THE MELANCHOLY OF MIKURU ASAHINA

All kinds of things had happened over the winter break, but stuff had turned out pretty much the way I'd expected, just like when you buy a lottery ticket and wind up not winning anything. The events of this story happened after I'd trudged up the hill to school again, cursing the school's cheap construction that made the bitterly cold weather seem even more bitterly cold.

Perhaps thanks to global warming, there hadn't been much snow, but that small favor was made up for by the fact that my classroom's lackluster heater seemed to keep the room's temperature roughly at the level of the South Pole. As I wondered if I'd be stuck with heaters like that until I graduated, I started to feel like I'd made a terrible mistake by picking North High, and I was ashamed of my junior high school self—but I was here now, so there was no helping it.

Today, as usual, I was headed to the SOS Brigade's headquarters in the clubroom building, to idle away the after-school hours.

The room had originally belonged to the literature club, but the previous year it had been annexed by the SOS Brigade for use as its hideout—it's hard to imagine a better example of giving someone an inch, only to have them take a mile. I got the feeling that the student body was beginning to forget there had ever been a literature club, and given Nagato's feelings as the sole member of said club, I wasn't inclined to worry about it too much. And if I wasn't worrying, you could bet Haruhi wasn't either.

In any case, this was where I went after school, and I had to admit I had nowhere else to go. Although I did occasionally consider ditching the brigade and going straight home, I would imagine a certain someone sitting behind me during class and staring killer laser beams at my back all day, and such fantasies would vanish like mist. This risk calculation was based on real-world experience, though whether that experience would help guide humanity down the right path, I had no idea.

Such things went through my mind as I arrived at the club-room door and knocked, as was my habit. If I just opened the door without any notice, there was a decent possibility that I would be greeted by a heavenly vision—but the knock was performed precisely to avoid that happening.

Going by the normal after-school routine, my knock would be answered by a soft "Come in!" and a beautiful second-year student so lovely you'd think she was an angel or a fairy or a spirit—take your pick—would open the door with a modest smile.

"—"

I waited, and waited some more—and there was no answer.

Which meant that not only was the resident angel/fairy/spirit not here, but neither was the board game–loving pretty boy; if someone were there, it would have to be the near-silent literature freak. And I was willing to bet just about anything except my own life on the fact that Haruhi wasn't there.

So I grasped the doorknob and opened the door as casually as I would open my refrigerator at home.

Haruhi was indeed not there. Nor was Koizumi. Not even Nagato.

However—

Asahina was there.

The petite, well-endowed second-year student wore her maid outfit, her profile as lovely as ever. She sat on a folding chair, hands grasping a broom as she sat there dazed, her mind elsewhere.

What could this be? Such a mood hardly suited her.

She didn't seem to have noticed that I'd entered the room as she stared off into space, a quiet sigh escaping her lips. Even her ennui was picture-perfect, like a scene from a movie that had required countless takes to capture. So nice.

After watching her for a while, I spoke up.

"Asahina?"

The effect was instantaneous.

"Huh? Oh, um, er—yes!"

Asahina jumped up from the chair, half standing, half sitting as she clutched the broom to her chest and looked at me with surprised eyes.

"Ah, Kyon! When did you...?"

When? After I knocked, I told her.

"Oh goodness, I didn't notice you at all... I-I'm sorry."

Her cheeks flushed with embarrassment and she hurriedly tried to explain.

"I was just thinking about... um... things. I'm sorry, really."

She hurried to put the broom away in the supply closet, then looked back to me. Her eyes were amazing. Everything about her was amazing. All hail Asahina! If I wasn't careful, I'd wind up just hugging her out of nowhere. It almost felt like I had to. Yes,

fine, I'd do it! No, wait, get a grip, Kyon. But just before the desperate battle between the angel and devil in my mind reached its conclusion —

"Where's Suzumiya? Isn't she with you?"

That was all it took to bring me back to reality. That was a close one. I nearly could've caused Haru-mageddon. I feigned calm and put my bag on the table.

"No, she's got classroom cleaning duty. She's probably sweeping dust all over the music room by now."

"I see…"

Asahina closed her lips, as though not terribly interested in Haruhi's whereabouts.

I couldn't help but wonder if something was up. Asahina definitely seemed strange. The girl from the future always greeted me with a smile like a single sunflower blooming in a vase (that part's a bit delusional) but at that moment, everything about her, from her fine features and soft hair to her obviously sweet breath, was overflowing with ennui.

Radiating unhappiness, Asahina stood directly before me, looking at me with her hands clasped and fingers intertwined. Despite whatever was troubling her, she seemed unsure of what to do about it. Perhaps unfortunately, she wasn't searching for the right words to confess her love. Though I wasn't searching for the memory, it came to me unbidden — the time I'd last seen her this way. It was the same expression she'd worn at Tanabata last year, when she'd asked me to go three years back in time with her (the first time).

It had been six months since then, and while Asahina was constantly improving her cuteness level, I remained as stupid as always. Nonetheless, as I tried to rein in Haruhi and the SOS Brigade a bit, I reflected on the fact that little by little I was starting to get used to it enough to tell myself, "Hey, this isn't so bad." I was sure nothing Asahina could tell me would really surprise me, and I had no intention of refusing her.

As I busied myself trying to burn the image of Asahina's maid-outfit-wearing countenance onto my retinas, she finally initiated conversation. Opening her always glossy lips, she spoke.

"Kyon, um...I need a favor..."

Ka-click.

The door made a quiet click, then slowly opened. What I saw as I reflexively looked behind me was a short-haired, expressionless girl who walked quietly into the room.

Nagato mechanically closed the door.

"..."

She took a glance at Asahina and me, then, like a ghost, walked over to her usual spot.

Emotionlessly, she took her seat, then produced a paperback book from her bag and opened it. She probably had no particular interest in the fact that Asahina and I stood facing each other midconversation, but if she did, it was evidently outweighed by the bulky, difficult-looking paperback.

Asahina's reaction was quicker, although far less subtle than mine would've been.

"Um...tea! I'll put on some tea."

She raised her voice as though wanting to announce her intentions, then trotted over to the kettle.

"Water, water—"

Holding the kettle, she trotted back over to the little refrigerator.

"Oh...we're out of water. I'll—I'll go get some."

Just as she was about to leave the clubroom, I stopped her.

"I'll get it," I said, offering to take the kettle. "It's cold outside, and you'll just tempt the other students in that outfit. We don't need to give a free show to nonmembers. The water fountain is just downstairs. I'll just run down there," I started to say, but—

"Oh, I'll go too!"

Asahina looked at me like a homeless kitten afraid of being abandoned on a rainy day. So cute. So cute, but also problematic.

Was she still not comfortable being left alone with Nagato? They probably needed to have a heart-to-heart, I thought, but maybe it was hard for an alien and a time traveler to talk to each other.

But that was fine with me. If Asahina wanted to stick with me instead of Nagato, you'd have to dig past the Mohorovicic discontinuity to find a reason for me to refuse her. I'd be surprised if one existed, although with Haruhi it was less certain, and I imagined she might be able to dig up some kind of oozy reason. Fortunately, Haruhi was not here, and I wouldn't find myself having a shovel forced on me.

I took the kettle and, unsure whether to sing or skip for joy, headed down the hall of the old building.

"Oh, wait for me—"

Asahina followed me in her maid outfit, like a kitten following its mother.

Although walking along with her like this was no special feat, pride swelled within me. Although I had not contributed to her looks, build, or personality, as far as I knew I was the only guy who regularly got close enough to touch her.

I was so proud, in fact, that I'd totally forgotten about the weird mood she'd been in earlier. Thus—

"Kyon—"

Asahina spoke as I started to fill the kettle with tap water.

"Are you free this Sunday? There's a place I'd like to go with you."

She sounded serious. I was stunned—no physical measuring device could possibly have measured my surprise. For a moment, I completely forgot what day it was and how many days there were before Sunday. With effort, I finally managed to speak.

"Of course I'm free."

Even if I'd had something to do on Sunday, an invitation from Asahina would turn a red-marked calendar totally blank. She could ask to meet on February twenty-ninth for all I cared—I'd still be there. Even if it wasn't a leap year, I'd find a way.

"Yeah, I'm free."

I forced the words out even as fumes began to seep up from within me.

I'd gotten an invitation like this before, I realized.

But the place we'd arrived at turned out to be three years in the past, and all that time travel got really old after a while. To be honest, it wasn't the kind of thing I wanted to do a lot. If I just up and did it all the time—which I wouldn't, but still—I'd get sick of it.

"Don't worry," said Asahina.

She looked down, unconsciously playing with the kettle lid in her hands. She watched the water flow out of the tap.

"We won't go to the past or the future. I, um…just want to buy some tea leaves at the mall. Will you help me pick some out, Kyon?"

She then dropped her voice, putting her finger to her lips and speaking barely above a whisper.

"But…keep this a secret from everyone, okay?"

It goes without saying that at that moment, I brimmed with confidence in my ability to resist any form of questioning.

Then came the waiting for Sunday. The minutes and seconds had never ticked by so slowly. Why did the hands of the clock move slower when you stared at them? Were they sneaking a break? I tried shaking the clock, but even that did nothing to speed up the hands, and it was then that I realized how powerless we humans are as we struggle in the face of eternal time.

This was my first outing with a time traveler that didn't involve any actual time travel. We were just going to buy tea leaves. I gave some thought to that. Naturally, I didn't think Asahina was some overprotected princess who couldn't do her own shopping, nor, clearly, did I think she was a shut-in who needed assistance to purchase tea. No matter how cheap the leaves were, I would gladly drink her tea, and it wasn't as though the SOS Brigade had any especially picky tea drinkers, anyway.

So why did she invite me along? And why so secretly?

A boy and a girl of similar age going out on a Sunday.

Wasn't that essentially what most people would call a "date"? Yes, it had to be. That was it. This was a date. The way I saw it, the tea thing had just been an excuse. How modest of her. She could have just come right out and asked. No, this was better — this was Asahina, after all.

Sunday finally arrived.

On my bike, I sprinted furiously to the agreed-upon station-front meeting place. The pedals revolved easily, even without a motor, as though my beloved bicycle understood my feelings. It wasn't an exaggeration to say that I was feeling as pleasant as I ever had since joining the SOS Brigade. This was just a normal outing. I wouldn't be closed up in some strange dimension, given a one-way ticket to the past, or discussing Zen riddles with an alien in her living room.

Of course, if the girl waiting for me in front of the station were Asahina the Elder, with her mysteriously knowing smile, that was another matter entirely.

I mean, I had a pretty average first-year high school student's brain. Given my experiences thus far, I could imagine the way the future might turn out. Asahina (the Elder) was part of it. I was sure I'd come across her again eventually, and if that were today, I wouldn't have been surprised.

"Aw, crap."

I muttered to myself as I left my bike in the shadow of a telephone pole.

My thoughts were starting to favor weirder explanations. At this rate, I wouldn't be surprised if something really did happen, and that lack of surprise itself would taint my sense of danger. You've got a few screws loose if you don't get surprised at things that should be surprising. I wanted to be a normal human, or at least preserve my sanity. I wanted to be able to laugh when I was supposed to laugh, even if I was a little late.

So I smiled hugely.

It was the usual Asahina who was standing at the SOS Brigade's traditional meeting place.

When I noticed her standing amid the weekend swell of traffic, waving at me with those small hands of hers, it was almost too much to bear.

Her outfit was chic and feminine, and her hair was done differently too—the subtle beauty of a girl making an effort to be grown-up and stylish. I was nearly moved to tears.

I stopped suddenly in front of the warmly dressed Asahina and gave her my best Koizumi smile, which I'd practiced many times in the mirror.

"Hi there. Sorry I'm late," I said, despite having arrived fifteen minutes early.

"Oh, no..."

Asahina breathed into her clasped hands—but her eyes were warm.

"I just got here myself..."

She smiled softly.

"Well, shall we go?"

I nodded quickly and took the first step.

Asahina's hair was tied up, exposing the nape of her neck; a feeling I found hard to name filled me. I walked like a knight sworn to protect a princess who was journeying to flee the internal strife of her family.

Her stride, like her features, seemed too youthful, and it was hard to believe she was really a year older than me. There was something childlike about her walk; it was like my younger sister's. Her unbalanced steps, so hard to imagine coming from a girl who was supposedly a second-year high school student, stirred up my protective instincts. When she occasionally looked up at me with her worried eyes, they conveyed an emotion that was hard to comprehend.

After all, the current activity was entirely out of the ordinary in a variety of ways. Normally we were in the clubroom with Haruhi or Nagato or Koizumi, and my emotions in that chaotic place swung between joy and sorrow.

But now it was just Asahina and me. And this was a secret from everyone else. The despotic brigade chief, omnipotent alien, and limited esper were nowhere to be found. How refreshing.

I felt like announcing it with all my strength. I am on an outing alone with Asahina, and I am incapable of responsible decisions!

To be honest, I was floating. Compared with the honor of walking side by side with the prettiest face of North High (by a wide margin), the Purple Ribbon was nothing; I would've happily chucked it into the ocean as fish food. Not that Japan would be crazy enough to give me an honor like that. Our destination was a shopping center near the station.

I occasionally came here to shop with my family. The buildings sold mostly clothing and food, though there was a large bookstore—but that was Nagato's territory, not mine. Unsurprisingly, Asahina led me to where the foodstuffs were sold.

We headed past a line of registers to an area that specialized in tea, with cases of a huge variety of Japanese-style green tea lined up in neat rows.

"Good afternoon!"

Asahina delivered a charming greeting, and the old man behind the counter cracked a smile like asphalt splitting on a hot day.

"Hey, welcome back!"

Evidently she was a regular customer.

"Hmm, which one should I get today...?"

Asahina murmured to herself, deep in thought as she gazed at the pots on which names and prices were handwritten.

It goes without saying that I don't know more about tea than she does, so I didn't try to give her any advice, instead simply staying at her side, my nose twitching at the unfamiliar scents of the various teas.

Asahina took her tea leaves seriously, and she talked passionately with the shopkeeper about things like how many times the leaves were dried and how long to let them steep, while I stood there uselessly like a scarecrow after the harvest.

No one in the SOS Brigade, including me, knew anything about tea. Haruhi would gulp down any vaguely colored liquid that was in a teacup, up to and including hydrogen peroxide. It wasn't even clear whether Nagato had taste buds. And Koizumi would never complain.

For my part, I was prepared to drink anything she prepared, even if it were a goblet full of hemlock. A promise was a promise. So long as I left myself in the care of a certain person afterward, I'd probably survive.

Being useless in the role of advisor, I stood guard next to Asahina in front of the store as she methodically picked out tea. Eventually she settled on a variety of green tea called something like "Master Wizard."

"We came all the way out here, after all..."

Asahina looked up at me with even more bashful eyes than usual.

"Would you like to have some of this tea with me? The snacks here are tasty too, and they'll let you brew tea you've just purchased."

Even in this store basement, there was a café with a little bit of seating. I wouldn't have refused even if the sun had exhausted its helium fuel. I happily followed Asahina, sitting down at a table to order dumplings and fine tea.

I was already starting to worry.

Asahina seemed to be very concerned with the time. She fidgeted constantly and kept stealing glances at her watch. Her actions seemed natural enough, so I doubted that she was doing it for my benefit—rather, she seemed to be trying to keep me from noticing—but unfortunately, I noticed. I mean, she kept checking her watch and letting these sad little sighs escape. It was impossible to ignore.

"These dumplings are tasty. Tea's good too. You've got great taste as usual, Asahina. Mmm, delicious."

I pretended not to notice. It was hard not to praise myself for being a considerate guy.

"Yeah…"

Asahina took a bite of her dumpling, then looked slowly down and checked her watch again.

My feeling that something was going on here continued to grow.

I'd been carried away all along. The notion of being able to go out with the unofficial Miss North High, whose legendary proportions were clear even in her adorable winter outfit, was enough to make me want to yell out my joy from the rooftop.

I sipped my tea; the hot liquid filtered down into my stomach as my suspicions grew.

There had to be a catch.

There was a large body of circumstantial evidence that pointed to the fact that Mikuru Asahina, the sole second-year student in the SOS Brigade, was a time traveler. For some reason, she had come to the past. Regardless of that reason, under Haruhi's tyranny she had become the SOS Brigade's mascot, a job that had nothing to do with her original duty.

Yes, her official assignment was to observe Haruhi and occasionally drag me into the past to fix certain events—yes, no matter how you looked at it, that was her job.

Today had to be something like that. The tea errand was some prologue to another incident. Did Asahina know that? Her worried expression and bearing were worrisome.

We finished our dumplings, and the time came to pay the check. Asahina strongly refused to let me contribute.

"No, it's fine. I'm the one who asked you along today. So let me—"

No, no, I couldn't possibly let you, I told her.

"It's okay, really! I mean, Kyon, you're always treating me…"

Well, that was because Haruhi had made the rule that whoever was last to assemble for a club meeting had to treat the whole club, and for some reason I was always last to arrive, but that was just the evil nature of the SOS Brigade. The situation here was totally different—we were practically on a date—and the cash in my wallet was dying to be freed.

"Please."

Asahina pleaded with me.

"Just let me."

She was so sincere, I found myself nodding.

Asahina and I left the mall, and with nowhere in particular to go, we found ourselves gazing at the passing crowds there beneath the cold midwinter sky.

When you're done with activities, normally you'd say, "Goodbye, see you tomorrow," but isn't that sort of lame? I wasn't cool or sociable enough to pull it off, and there was still a good amount of time before the sun would set. We were only a month into winter—the sun was only just starting to set early.

As I was trying to decide where to ask her to go, she beat me to it.

"Would you accompany me for a little walk? Please, Kyon."

Again with those pleading eyes. That face and voice could turn anyone's legs into jelly; I was powerless to resist.

Asahina smiled mistily.

"This way. Shall we?"

She started walking without hesitation. I had hoped she would take my arm, but unfortunately that seemed too high a hope.

Shrugging my shoulders in the chilly air, I followed the petite second-year student.

We walked for some time after that.

She seemed to have a destination in mind, occasionally glancing at me to confirm I was still there beside her as she walked.

I was realizing more and more that something was strange about her today, but I said nothing as I strolled along with her.

How to put it? Asahina's usual mode was funnier, charming all around with her adorable mannerisms, but today she was like Taniguchi or me as we trudged up the hill to school on the day of a physics exam.

And on top of that, she kept peering around us.

It was like she thought she was being followed . . . no, that wasn't it. Whatever she was worried about wasn't behind her. She seemed to be concerned about her front arc. Glancing around like an elementary schooler who'd missed an orienteering checkpoint on a field trip, she looked like either a criminal or a tourist. If she had been a middle-aged man instead of a fetching lass, she probably would have been questioned by a passing patrol car. But with her charms, she would probably be pardoned of any offense. Not that any of that mattered.

Maybe her suspicious manner was why I wasn't paying attention to anything else.

I realized I was feeling somehow nostalgic, and I started to slow down.

It was a strange feeling—I'd played around this neighborhood my entire life, and the scenery was entirely familiar to me, so why—

"Ah."

My breath caught in my mouth at the understanding. I see.

I suddenly understood why the path we'd taken from the station had felt so familiar, as well as where this strange nostalgia came from.

It would be hard to forget the day last May when the SOS Brigade conducted its first citywide search for mysterious phenomena. The memory of Asahina and me walking aimlessly together after having drawn straws and getting paired together was engraved particularly deeply upon my mind, and I doubt I will ever forget it as long as I live.

And we were now walking down that same path. The nostalgia came from the situation—walking that same way, again with Asahina. Not even a year had passed since then, but it felt like the distant past. After all, I now knew for certain that Asahina was a time traveler, but back then I hadn't had a clue. Until I heard her shocking statements on the bench beneath the cherry blossoms, I'd thought she was just an ordinary, if well-endowed, girl.

But all that was gone now. It was in the past. No wonder I was feeling nostalgic.

As I expected, Asahina was heading to the place where the memories were thickest. Only this time, she was glancing around like a nervous herbivore upon the grasslands, and she was still constantly checking her watch.

Her strange behavior continued; I knew better than to expect a response if I spoke up.

We continued to walk, our breath constantly white in the winter air, until finally we reached the place.

The cherry trees beside the river.

The Yoshino cherry trees along this path had bloomed twice last year—in the spring and again in the fall. I just hoped they had enough life in them to bloom again the coming spring.

I was feeling rather emotional, but Asahina didn't seem to care. Even when we passed the bench where she'd delivered her explosive revelation, she didn't seem to notice at all. She was the very embodiment of absentmindedness. What was she so worried about?

As I rather desolately tried to guess, she suddenly sighed to herself.

"Isn't it time yet...?"

She checked her watch.

"It should happen any moment now...but..."

She didn't seem to realize she'd spoken as she let out another sigh again, then looked around.

I pretended not to notice and concentrated on walking.

Great. Any idea that this had been a date now seemed like a distant memory. I'd hoped for a more relaxed, romantic stroll, but clearly it was not meant to be. I guess that's life.

We didn't see so much as a leaf, to say nothing of an actual flower petal, and soon the desolate cherry trees were behind us.

Asahina was heading upstream. If we kept going, we'd reach another memorable place—Nagato's apartment. If we continued even farther, we'd wind up going all the way back to North High.

Thanks to all the walking, my body was warming up—apparently not all of the warmth was coming from the girl next to me.

Eventually we descended down off the riverbank and made for the train tracks. We walked along the private rail line; I'd once walked this way with Haruhi too.

With all the memories surfacing in my mind, even I started to feel a little uneasy.

"Kyon, this way."

"Huh?"

If Asahina hadn't tugged on my sleeve, I would have just kept going.

"We need to cross the street."

We were at the intersection of the tracks and the street. Asahina was pointing to the pedestrian crossing signal for the prefectural road, which flashed a red DON'T WALK message.

"Oh, sorry."

I apologized and lined myself up next to her. Though the street was quiet and free from cars, it was very Asahina-like of her to insist on waiting anyway.

We didn't have to wait more than ten seconds. The traffic light flicked from green to yellow, then soon lit up red, and in exchange, the pedestrian signal turned green.

I took my first step almost simultaneously with Asahina.

And then—

A little shadow rushed past me from behind.

"Ah—"

It was Asahina who cried out in a small voice.

The shadow ran past me and through the crosswalk, toward the other side. It was an elementary school boy, about the same age as my sister, maybe fourth or fifth grade. He wore glasses and had an intelligent look about him.

"Aah!"

It was Asahina again who shouted, and the shout reached my ears along with a terrible noise that made my eyes snap wide open.

A car was speeding toward the crossing, its tires squealing. The traffic signal was red. Nevertheless, the car—a moss-green minivan—was heading toward the crosswalk with no sign of deceleration.

Then—

The kid who had sprinted into the street realized he was in danger and froze.

The car was closing in. The driver had about as much respect for the speed limit as he or she had for the red light. A premonition of the kid flying through the air flashed through my mind, and before I realized what was happening, my body was in motion.

"You stupid son of a—"

I didn't know whether I was yelling at the car or the kid, but I ran. It felt like everything was in slow motion. I'm sure from a third-person perspective it all happened in an instant.

"Whoa—!"

I made it. I grabbed the glasses-wearing kid by the collar and pushed him back with all my strength, the force of which carried me to safety as well.

The speeding car disappeared almost instantly.

I was covered in sweat.

It had been close. The van's tires had passed by my toes with millimeters to spare. A step later, and everything from my ankles down would've been as flat as a worn-out shoe.

"That crazy bastard!"

I didn't know who'd been driving, but blood rushed to my head as I raged at the escaping car.

"What the hell kind of driving was that? Speeding through a red light? Is he trying to get somebody killed? Asahina, did you get his plates?"

I'd missed them, having been busy tumbling over with the boy. Hoping her vision had been good, I looked up to her—

"So this was it…"

What?

Asahina stood rooted to the spot, eyes wide. That wasn't what surprised me, though—it was hardly surprising that she'd be stunned after witnessing such a close call.

No, what surprised me was that the expression on Asahina's face wasn't merely one of shock.

"So that's why… I see. That's why I was called here…"

Asahina murmured to herself, looking at the boy who'd very nearly been hit.

The expression of surprise on her beautiful face was mixed with a strange understanding.

Without the slightest idea of what was going on, I kept my rear glued to the ground until eventually Asahina stiffly came over to us, her face pale. Unfortunately, she was not heading toward me, but rather to the boy, who was also sitting on the ground.

The boy's face was also sheet-white, probably from the shock of the near miss. His eyes blinked rapidly at Asahina.

"Are you all right?"

She knelt down on the asphalt, placing her hands on the boy's shoulders. He nodded rapidly.

"Can you tell me your name?"

I had no idea why she needed to know his name, but the boy answered her.

I'd never heard the name before. But Asahina had, it seemed.

The instant she heard his name, she seemed to stop breathing. Doing a great impression of Nagato, she unblinkingly looked the boy in the eye for a long moment, then finally took a deep breath and spoke.

"I see...so you're..."

The boy's mouth hung open. Having escaped death by runaway minivan, now a beautiful girl was staring him in the eye and asking his name. It was enough to stun anyone. I knew how the poor kid felt.

But Asahina was serious.

"Listen, you have to promise me."

Her face was tight, in a way I'd never seen in the clubroom.

"From now on...you have to look out for cars, okay? When you're crossing the street or getting in a vehicle, or even on an airplane or a train, you have to be careful. Boats, too. So you don't get hurt or run over, or fall or sink. Always be careful, okay? I want you to promise me."

The boy was shocked. I know I was. There was no need to say all that stuff. It just seemed like it was going overboard.

"Please…"

Asahina's moist-eyed entreaty was enough to make even me want to shout, "Yes, ma'am!" And just as I was about to—

"Okay."

The boy nodded. Even if he didn't understand why, he seemed to see that it was important to her. He looked at her closely.

"I'll be careful."

He spoke flatly, then ducked his head, bobbing like a roly-poly toy whose balance has been disturbed.

Asahina didn't seem satisfied by that, and she extended the pinky of one hand.

"Let's make a pinky promise, then."

Watching the boy tentatively link pinkies with Asahina caused a twinge in the corners of my chest. I believe it was what you call "jealousy." Selfishly, I wanted her to do that only with me. But, hell, he was just a kid, and I wasn't so immature as to fake falling over just to get in their way—but neither was I enough of an adult not to feel some relief when she finally stood up. I don't know if that was a good thing or not.

As an alternative, I looked up at the signal.

"Asahina, the light's about to change. We should get out of the road."

The crosswalk signal had started to flash.

"Oh, yes."

Asahina finally stood, but she continued to gaze at the boy, who was smart enough to finally notice this. He bowed.

"Thank you very much for saving me. I'll be careful from now on."

He then added a bow to his words.

"Excuse me, and 'bye!"

He bowed again, then scampered off across the road at full speed.

Asahina didn't move. She watched the boy as though he were a precious gem, as he ran off into the distance with the peculiar quickness of a child.

I couldn't take it anymore.

"Asahina, the light's red. C'mon—"

I pulled the winter-clothed beauty out of the street and back onto the walking path. Her complacent body was as relaxed as Shamisen's when he randomly decided to curl up in my bed. I knew she would be very soft if I decided to hug her—not that I did, of course.

Just as the light turned red—

"Ooh…"

I heard a sob come from diagonally behind me. It was coming from Asahina, and it was muffled—she had shoved her face into my arm.

Huh? I thought.

Asahina buried her face even deeper, and her shoulders were shaking. It didn't seem likely that she was laughing.

She continued to sob.

Transparent liquid dripped from her eyes onto my clothing, soaking into it. She clung to me like a child as her tears overflowed.

"Wh-what is it? Asahina, um, are you—"

I'd been in a few impossible situations in the past, but this was on an entirely different level. Why was she crying? We'd saved the boy, hadn't we? Nobody had died—shouldn't she be happy instead of sad? Was it just a reaction to the shock of the sudden danger?

"No, that's not it."

Asahina answered through her sniffling.

"…I'm so pathetic. I don't understand anything…I can't do anything."

Well, now I didn't understand anything.

But she just kept crying, apparently having lost all will to articulate coherent thoughts. Like the way Shamisen clawed onto me when I picked him up, she grabbed onto my clothes with both hands, burying her face in my sleeve.

What was going on here?

My mind whirled with questions, but only one answer was forthcoming.

The day's events were over. The pseudo-date she'd invited me out on, the mysterious walk we'd taken — it was all over now.

I didn't have to be Koizumi to deduce that much.

I couldn't very well stand there beneath the freezing sky all day while a distressed upperclassman clung to me.

There were eyes on the walking path, and several people stared at the strange couple as they passed, wondering what the two could possibly be doing on a cold day like this.

"Asahina, maybe we should go somewhere to sit down. Um… can you walk?"

Her face still pressed against my upper arm, but I saw her chestnut hair nod.

I slowly started to walk, matching my stride to Asahina's unsteady steps. Accompanied by the sniffling, clinging girl, progress was slow — it was both what I'd wished for and not. The one thing I hoped for now was that no boys from our school saw us. If they did, the probability that I'd be targeted by the Mikuru Asahina followers would spike.

"Where shall we go?"

We needed someplace where we could rest out of sight. A respite from the cold would be nice too. My first thought was a café, but sitting across from a sobbing lass in a café didn't sound particularly comfortable.

A while ago, I'd noticed one building that was in the direction we were heading — it was Nagato's swanky apartment. I was sure she'd let us in if we asked, but something told me that wasn't a great idea.

So there was only one place left—we were getting close to the
mecca for weirdos that was in Nagato's neighborhood, that place
where so many of my memories lay sealed away—yes, the park.
We'd already passed the bench by the river, so it only made sense
to try the other spot where so much had happened.

At least we would be able to sit down. And who knew, maybe
somebody would pop out from the bushes behind us.

It seemed that people willing to visit the park in this freezing
weather were in the minority. The bench I'd been thinking of
was unoccupied and exposed to the wind, as though we'd
obtained reserved tickets for it ahead of time.

I sat Asahina down, then sat down next to her at a slight
remove. Glancing at her profile, I saw her looking down, a few
tears still clinging to her cheeks.

Searching my pockets for a handkerchief, all I felt was the fab-
ric of my clothes. Damn, of all the days to forget it! Just as I was
despairing of finding any other cloth to wipe her tears with and
considering ripping off my own sleeve—

Whump.

I felt a soft pressure on my shoulder and looked to see that it
was Asahina's forehead. It looked like she was going to continue
her crying jag there. My shoulder was suddenly itchy. It was like
when someone puts their finger close to the spot between your
eyes—your skin gets the wrong idea. Something like that. Of
course, I was actually being touched, so I must have been pretty
worn-out.

"Want me to get you a cup of coffee?"

I thought it was a fine idea, but the head of chestnut hair shook
in the negative.

"What about some oolong tea?"

Again the forehead pressed to my shoulder shook left to right,
a bit peevishly.

I tried to picture the menu from the nearby vending machine.

"What about—"

"I'm sorry."

Her weak voice finally reached my ears. With her face still against my shoulder, I couldn't see her expression. But I didn't need to. She only apologized when she was really, genuinely sorry.

I decided not to say anything, and I waited for her to continue.

"The reason I asked you along was to save that boy. I didn't know before, but now I do. That was it. That was all."

By all means, continue.

"I...I asked you out on the orders of my superiors. The places we went, the paths we took, the timing—it was all on their orders, so we would be able to save that boy...That was my duty."

Her superiors, huh? Asahina the Elder's smile flashed through my mind.

"Can I just ask something? Why don't those so-called superiors of yours give you a little more detail? Like just go to a certain intersection and protect so-and-so at a certain time."

"Um...I wish they would tell me too. But it's no good. They won't tell me anything. I'm sure it's because I'm not good enough. All I can do is follow orders. Just like today—"

I thought again of the elder Asahina and that smile of hers.

"I'm sure that's not true..."

In response to my assurance, her chestnut hair gave the biggest shake of the day so far.

"No, it is! They'd never give me such an important mission without any details otherwise! Why...it's just..."

Her crying came back in full force. I had to change the subject.

"Who was that kid, anyway?"

Asahina sniffled for a while before answering.

"...He is a very important person for us in the future. He's the reason we're able to be in this time period. He must continue to exist…"

Her voice got quieter and quieter.

"…I can't say more…I'm sorry…"

In other words, that kid—whoever he was—could not be allowed to die. In order to prevent his accident, Asahina was directed to bring me to this place.

If I'd been a second slower in catching the glasses-wearing brat, he would've been hit head-on by that speeding minivan. I don't know what would've happened to him after that, but it probably would've been the worst possible outcome. Short of a miracle, he would've said sayonara to his world.

"Hmm?"

Wait a second—which history was the right one? I'd saved the boy. That was reality now. So what about the future? Did the future Asahina come from the one where the boy had been hit? And to avoid that, Asahina had used me to save him—

No, that didn't make sense either.

My saving him meant that the kid narrowly avoiding his accident was now historical fact. So that had to hold true for the future too. Otherwise, it meant that Asahina's future was discontinuous from the present. So in that case, from the perspective of the future, the kid hadn't had an accident, so why bother going all the way back to the past to prevent it—but unless they did so, he would have an accident…

"Ouch."

My head hurt.

Something was wrong. Whenever I tried to think about hard stuff like this, I felt like smoke was pouring from my ears.

"I don't understand."

I spoke the truth.

"I don't see which one is the correct reality—the kid having the accident or surviving it?"

Shaking her head hesitantly, Asahina spoke in a voice like a droplet of water.

"We are not the only ones who have come from the future. There are others who do not wish for our future to exist. So..."

The moss-green minivan. The insane driver.

"Do you mean..."

My memories all screamed the same thing at me.

Ryoko Asakura, for one. She was from a different faction within the Data Overmind.

There was another organization besides Koizumi's "Agency." I remembered him jokingly saying something about a secret struggle taking place.

And there was another, much more recent memory. The creator of that house we'd encountered in the mountains. It had been a mysterious dimension that even Nagato couldn't analyze. "An enemy of the SOS Brigade," Koizumi had called it.

Which one of those had done this? Our enemy. I didn't like that word.

They had tried to erase a boy who had originally needed to live. Which meant that his existence was a problem for them.

Others, who do not wish for our future to exist—

Who were they? I asked.

"That's..."

Asahina's lip trembled. She tried to speak, but her face soon showed her surrender.

"...I can't tell you now. Not...not yet."

She was shifting back to crying mode.

"That's what's so pathetic. Really. I can't do anything. I can't even help you understand."

That wasn't true.

Asahina wasn't useless at all. She was just being prevented from doing anything. And the one doing it was her future self, Asahina the Elder.

But I couldn't say that.

During the first Tanabata incident, I'd sat right here on this very bench and promised her I wouldn't. I'd even pinky-promised.

"You have to keep me a secret from her," she'd said.

How long I'd have to keep the secret, I had no idea. And if I didn't know, I shouldn't tell her. I didn't understand it myself. I just felt very strongly that I shouldn't say anything.

I wasn't sure how my silence was being interpreted, but Asahina spoke in a quiet voice.

"Even before, you were the one who saved that boy, right? It's strictly prohibited for people from the future to interfere directly."

Oh, really?

"The only ones who may change the past are those who live within it. Anything else is against the rules…"

Hence my debut.

"I just did what my superiors told me to do, without knowing anything. I didn't know why I was doing any of it. When I think about it, it just makes me feel so…stupid."

That wasn't true.

"I've written messages, trying to get them to let me tell you more…but they are always rejected. It's because I'm so useless, I just know it."

That wasn't true either.

I finally opened my mouth.

"You're not useless. Really—you've done so much for me, for the SOS Brigade, and for the world. You shouldn't worry about it like this."

Asahina looked up suddenly, but soon she pointed her tearful eyes back down.

"But all I ever do is wear a bunch of different outfits…" Her voice was low. "And even then, I didn't know anything…" It rose again.

By "then" she meant December eighteenth—

"You're wrong."

I was about as serious as I ever get. Asahina seemed to realize that, and she looked up at me, surprised.

Asahina was no mere teatime maid mascot. The buxom beauty that she would become appeared in my mind.

Snow White. She had given me the hint that had allowed me to return with Haruhi from closed space.

Tanabata, three years ago. After traveling back in time with Asahina, I'd gone to Asahina the Elder, who'd sent me to the waiting Nagato.

And she'd helped me restore history after it had been altered.

Oh, right, I haven't talked about that incident yet. It's a long story, so I'll try to keep it brief, but to sum things up, it was right after the winter field trip that we'd done it. Nagato, Asahina, and I had gone back in time to then, where we'd met a dying version of myself along with Nagato's transformed version before putting everything in order. Asahina should have remembered that much, but what she wouldn't notice (unlike Nagato and me) was the future version of herself. Asahina the Elder had made sure of that.

What was certain was that they were both Asahina — unlike the Asahina in the alternate timeline, who didn't recognize me. To put it Nagato's way, they were temporal variations of the same entity.

This Asahina was only acting on the orders of her boss, that much was clear, and I was sure that boss was in fact Asahina the Elder. The adult Asahina knew exactly what her younger self did and did not know. They were the same person, after all.

If there was something this Asahina needed to know, the elder Asahina would have long since told me what it was. The fact that she hadn't meant that there was nothing I could say. "You must not tell her who was there," Asahina the Elder had made me promise.

True enough, I could easily just tell her that an even lovelier version of herself had come from farther in the future to help me. It would be just as easy as it would have been to wake the other version of myself after I'd come back from my second trip back in time and tell him everything. But I hadn't done that, of course, and he hadn't done that to me. And because he hadn't done that to me, it was something I couldn't do. Instead, I did only what I had to do.

This Asahina would someday return to the future. Then she would travel back in time again, older this time, to help us. It was true that at the moment her calling seemed to be to serve as the SOS Brigade's lovely maid, but that didn't mean she was useless. Everything was connected. The future would happen because of the present. If the elements were altered, the future would naturally change.

Thinking on all this, I suddenly realized something.

"Oh!"

I wanted to say it. But I couldn't. I couldn't. But I felt like I could finally put a name to this itchy feeling.

I thought about the previous summer, during the brigade's first hunt for mysterious phenomena. I'd walked along with Asahina, and there beneath the cherry blossoms she'd told me she was from the future and explained the principles of time travel, although whether that incredible lecture about time planes was really an explanation or not wasn't clear.

Back then, no matter what I asked her, she'd always given me the same answer.

"That's classified."

What I was feeling now was surely the same thing she'd felt then. I couldn't tell her.

"Asahina."

I still wanted to tell her something.

"Yes?"

Asahina gazed up at me with big, wet eyes.

"Um...look. You're...how do I put this...you're not just some toy for Haruhi—er...huh. Like, there's another layer, or like a background...thing. Hmm..."

I trailed off, my thought unfinished as I failed to find the right words. It was no good; no matter what I said, I ran into something I shouldn't say. It was damn annoying. I couldn't think of words that would comfort her but also be safe to say. I'm sure if Koizumi were here, he'd be able to condense a whole lecture into a dozen words. But I had to keep myself from always running to him or Nagato for help. This was my problem.

But just like giving a computer to a monkey doesn't mean he can use it, my mind couldn't conjure up the vocabulary I needed to abandon the status quo.

"Um...look..."

Thinking some physical stimulation might get the ol' neurons firing, I knocked on my head with my fists. And yet—

"Er...uh..."

I just wound up rubbing my temples as I groaned.

Until Asahina spoke.

"Kyon, it's okay."

I looked up and met her glittering eyes, but they were definitely smiling now.

"It's okay, really."

She repeated herself.

"I understand. What you're trying to—"

She understood? What did she understand? I didn't even know what I was trying to say.

"You don't have to say anything. It's enough."

Asahina's once-closed lips opened, her gaze full of kindness. In her eyes there was a faint but unmistakably gentle understanding.

I finally got it.

What, you ask? Wasn't it obvious?

I had realized that she had realized.

Perhaps she'd understood from my stuttering manner what I couldn't plainly tell her. It was something that would take her feeling of powerlessness and throw it far, far away. But I couldn't say it. So what could it be? There weren't many possible answers.

"Oh—"

As soon as I opened my mouth, Asahina calmly moved her hand. Something at once cold and warm touched my lips—it was her index finger, cutting off what I was about to say.

It was enough.

There was no need to say any more. She had received the message I couldn't send. I understood that. There was silence between us.

"Mmm."

Asahina slowly removed her finger, then put it to her own lips. She winked clumsily.

"Yeah."

I left it at that.

We didn't need any words. It was true. No pitcher in the world had to call out his pitches to the catcher. The world was full of convenient signals. If you didn't need words to convey a simple message, then why use them?

There were other ways of communication that more than sufficed.

I wondered if that wasn't perhaps a special property of emotions. Think about it—we shared sympathy without words. So there wasn't any need to say more. Words were superfluous. Saying more than necessary was meaningless, a waste of breath.

Asahina smiled.

I returned her smile.

That was enough. Our feelings made up for what our words couldn't say.

The next day—Monday.

After school, everybody gathered in the SOS Brigade head-

quarters as usual, and after drinking the tea Asahina and I had bought just the previous day, the brigade chief spoke up.

"So, Kyon."

I had taken care to enjoy the tea more than usual, while Haruhi, who had never learned about being thankful, downed the entire scalding cup in three seconds. One hundred grams of that stuff cost six hundred yen—it wouldn't have killed her to savor it a little.

"What?" I answered, glancing at the smiling Asahina, goddess among maids, out of the corner of my eye.

"Oh, would you like more tea?"

Just as Asahina hurried to pour more tea into Haruhi's empty cup—

Haruhi leaned forward from the reclining position she'd assumed in her brigade chief's chair, then rested her chin atop her clasped hands, her elbows on the table, and said a strange thing.

"I have this strange habit of talking to myself."

Did she now? I never knew. This was the first I'd heard of it in close to a year.

"I don't even pay attention to the people around me when I do it."

Well, you should probably get that looked at before someone decides to publish a collection of your "wisdom," I thought.

"So I'm just gonna talk to myself for a while. You'll probably hear me, but don't worry about it."

Before I could point out how stupid that was, Haruhi started talking in a strangely casual voice.

"So a little ways from my house, there's this really smart kid. He wears these glasses like a miniature professor, and he's got a super clever-looking face. His name's—"

Haruhi mentioned a name I had definitely heard recently. My back broke out in a sweat, and it wasn't because of the heat.

Just as she was tilting the teapot to pour, Asahina froze.

Haruhi seemed unaffected, and she continued.

"Aaaanyway, sometimes I help the little guy study. Like yesterday, for example. And so he says to me, 'I saw the bunny girl with a boy.'"

Haruhi assumed a truly unpleasant grin.

"Apparently he saw us when we were doing location shoots for the movie last autumn, and he really remembered seeing Mikuru in her bunny outfit. And so while we were on the subject, I asked him what the boy she was with looked like. And here's the composite sketch."

From somewhere, Haruhi produced a piece of paper torn from a notebook. On it was a rough but relatively skillful sketch of— hmm, somehow it looked like the face I saw every morning in the mirror. I mean, it was me, definitely.

"Heh heh heh."

Haruhi laughed meaningfully.

That talky brat was surprisingly good at drawing. Wasn't he supposed to become a scientist or something in the future? Was he aiming to be an artist? If I'd known, I would've bought him off to still his wagging tongue and scribbling hands.

My gaze swam for about three seconds as I held out hope that someone would come and save me.

Asahina simply stood there and trembled, her voice having apparently lost all function. It seemed very unlikely that a new character would burst into the clubroom, so my options were limited.

"..."

My eyes met Nagato's, which had warmed to about minus-four degrees Celsius. For some reason, my stomach hurt.

Meanwhile, Koizumi wore a little half smile, as though he was going to enjoy sitting this one out. Wait a sec—did these two know everything? Were they just going to sit there?

"So?"

Haruhi spoke with an expression that looked like she'd just downed a finely crushed mix of chili powder and psychedelic mushrooms—that is to say, somehow bulge-eyed yet also like she was finding something indescribably funny.

"I want you to tell me exactly what you did and where you went with Mikuru yesterday. Don't worry, I won't get mad."

I looked at Asahina out of the corner of my eye; she was turning so pale that if she went any further, she'd look like a tree frog drenched in blue paint; for my part, I was sweating like a toad surrounded by three dozen anacondas.

I seem to remember some kind of hallucination. Haruhi's primary-colored aura taking some sort of fighting shape and slamming into an invisible wall behind Nagato, shattering into fireworks—or something like that.

"Pardon me."

Koizumi stood up as if wanting to avoid the invisible fireworks, and he picked up his chair, moving it toward the windowpane.

Then, as if to say, "By all means, please continue," he spread out his hands and gave a benevolent smile.

Damn you, Koizumi! I'd get him back for this. Maybe in a high-stakes game of Seven Bridge. Just you remember this.

"Um…er…"

So, what sort of lie did I need to tell? I didn't have a lot of time, so any help would have been very much appreciated. A telegram would have been best; express mail would not have been fast enough.

As I muttered, Haruhi put it to me again.

"Spit it out! All the way through to the end, nice and simple so Yuki and Koizumi and I can all understand it. Or else…"

Haruhi took a deep breath, then assumed a deliberate smile.

"…I'll give you two a punishment unlike anything you've ever seen before! Let's see, how about…this!"

The punishment that Haruhi smoothly laid out made falling to hell sound vastly preferable; Asahina and I could only look at each other and tremble.

There's no need to waste words on what happened in the clubroom after that.

Faced with Haruhi's unnatural, unpleasant grin, Nagato's colder-than-usual gaze, and Koizumi's amused spectating, I searched desperately for an excuse, any excuse, like a man trying to wring water from a sponge left out to dry in the desert, while beside me Asahina clutched the kettle and tea container, cowering desperately.

I really don't think I need to say any more.

AFTERWORD

Originally this volume was supposed to be a long-form story, but that got unscrupulously abandoned, and this collection of short- and medium-length pieces wound up getting put out instead. The pattern so far is long, long, short, long, short, and the addition of another short collection means we've established a kind of heterogeneous repetition, but it's a total coincidence, so don't read anything into it.

"LIVE ALIVE"

It always bugged me that with all the buildup to the school festival, we never got to see the festival itself, so eventually the urge to turn the story I'd been thinking about into actual written words caught up with me. Either way, Haruhi is the main character in this one.

"THE ADVENTURES OF MIKURU ASAHINA EPISODE 00"

Will we do *The Revenge of Yuki Nagato Episode 00*, followed by *The Awakening of Itsuki Koizumi Episode 00* to complete the trilogy? I can't really say. I guess I just wanted to try my hand at directing. There's neither hide nor hair of Haruhi in this story.

"LOVE AT FIRST SIGHT"

This happens after *Disappearance* but before "Snowy Mountain Syndrome." I love American football, and I watch quite a bit of it, but it's hardly ever on broadcast TV in Japan, so I often wind up knowing the results before I can see the games, which is too bad. Nagato's definitely front and center in this one.

"WHERE DID THE CAT GO?"

I wound up writing this story because Koizumi mentioned the cat in "Snowy Mountain Syndrome." I worked seriously on this one because I wanted to give people something to think over. Somehow it feels like Haruhi and Tsuruya are the main characters here.

"THE MELANCHOLY OF MIKURU ASAHINA"

Chronologically speaking, the next long-form volume will follow directly after this story. Fortunately, thanks to my slaving away to connect the short magazine pieces to the longer stories I'd already written, this new long section is proving easier to write, but the important thing is whether or not it will be easy to read, and that's all I wish for, truly.

Thus has the sixth volume of this series come to pass, and for that I am both honored and deeply grateful. It is only thanks to the assistance of many people, along with the ongoing support of the readers, that this book exists. They have my deepest thanks.

See you again.

Nagaru Tanigawa

THE
WAVERING
OF
HARUHI
SUZUMIYA

Illustration by Noizi ITO

HARUHI GRINNED

UNPLEASANTLY.

THE PATH RAN BESIDE THE LINE OF CHERRY TREES NEXT TO THE RIVER. ASAHINA WALKED SILENTLY ALONG IT.